Buoy in the Fog

Spanning the globe, dodging death,
Jack searches for his perfect love

D1542250

M. Wagner

outskirts
press

Outskirts Press, Inc.
http://www.outskirtspress.com

ISBN: 978-1-9772-6143-4

Cover illustrated by Victor Guiza © 2023 M. Wagner

Outskirts Press and the "OP" logo are trademarks belonging to Outskirts Press,
Inc.

PRINTED IN THE UNITED STATES OF AMERICA

CONTENTS

REFLECTION

A bird chirped followed by the soft scratching sound of squirrels climbing on the red cedar tree came through the opened window. Usually a light sleeper and early-riser, but this morning his sleep had been deep. Instead of grasping at the dream images and trying to get back to them after turning over, a musical phrase was softly playing in his head ...

"Baa dip datt dodily doo"

A very slight puff of moist Atlantic air came through the window and he opened his right eye to peer through it. The nightstand clock read 5:32 am, earlier than his usual rising time. He glanced back again to the open window and saw the fog. Peering across the front yard of rolling grass and Red Cedar trees, the fog clung to the surface of the pond water like a puffy cotton blanket.

It wasn't the normal pattern to get fog in mid-July on Long Islands' Cold Spring Pond in Southampton. But this fog, he thought, was interesting.

1

Rolling onto his back, the big dog at the foot of the bed moaned but gave way to the turning of his feet and legs. Eyes closed again, those stray notes played softly ... a jazz phrase from last night? ... an accidental collision of intervals and timing? ... probably not, but it beckoned to Jack just the same.

As if it were a visible wisp of smoke that waved and danced through the air in a rhythmic sultry way, wet with sex ... ***"Baa dip datt dodily doo"*** ... he could almost see it ... a little trill of something with an unexpected pause that popped in a delightful lick.

"Damn!" he breathed, *"That is neat."*

Lifting the sheet, he swung his feet to the floor and sat a moment. To his right, at the foot of the bed lay the slumbering Rottweiler. A pat on the head resulted in a guttural *"Mummph"* acknowledgement.

"Good boy, Argus. Protect the mommy-unit for me," He whispered, stroking the big blocky head. *"Mummph"* the dog answered still nestled in sleep and wanting to stay undisturbed, but now had an eye half-open.

He named the dog "Argus" after Odysseus faithful canine companion. In his version of the story, Odysseus had to leave for an extended period of

time and entrusted Argus to protect the home
and his beautiful wife, Penelope. As he usually did,
Odysseus hugged Argus and instructed him to be
ever vigilant. But many years passed, Argus watched
and waited every day, until disguised as a beggar,
Odysseus slipped in a back gate of his estate. The
old dog, white with age, recognized his master and
struggled to rise. Odysseus dropped to his knees
and embraced him. A moment passed, then Argus
expired having fulfilled his duty to his master.

"Baa dip datt dodily doo"

It compelled him to figure it out before it
dissipated ... play it again and again, to understand
it, to know it fully and able to put it into an
improvisational flurry of notes. He needed to
grab one of his saxophones and give it a toot. He
was driven to figure out the note intervals, pace
fingerings and how to "color" the saxophone's
growl. But, it was too early to wake the
inhabitants of the surrounding cottages.

He stood up and peered out at the fog again and
then looked at the two of them still deep asleep
in the bed. Samantha's youthful, pixie-like face
was surrounded by the swirled mass of blond hair.
Her face wouldn't look very happy waking at this
hour, nor would her ever protective beast, Argus.
He loves them so completely ... the woman of his
dreams ... and her faithful protector.

The all white room with white trim, tan carpet and light colored furniture, typical of the popular Hamptons interior style, was easy to navigate in low light to get his clothes from the chair across the room.

He pulled on a T-shirt and cargo shorts before slipping out the bedroom door closing it gently behind.

In the kitchen, grinding some coffee beans, it struck him to take their small boat out with one of his horns ... maybe far enough from shore to avoid waking or annoying anyone.

"Baa dip datt dodily doo"

He poured water into the machine and glanced at the calendar hanging on the refrigerator door.

"Oh yeah, Aunt Martha," he muttered, remembering the wake for his mom's sister later that afternoon up-island. His mother had passed on six years ago at 80 years young and her older sister had just passed last week.

As the water dripped into the pot, he left the kitchen. In the bathroom, he caught a glimpse of the face in the mirror. *"Jack! What happened to you? You look like shit!"* Crow's feet, grey roots at his hairline and goatee were beginning to reveal

the deceit of hair and beard colorings that hid
the inevitable gray. It seemed to him it was only
yesterday he sported a curly brown mop. *"This is
happening all too soon. I'm just a few years shy of
retirement."*

He stopped in the dining room on the way back
to the kitchen. The early-American hutch in the
middle of the room was full of memories ... old
bottles he had found while scuba diving, serving
platters from his parents, knick-knack interesting
things from the 1900s to World War II ... a funky
hodge-podge of time that somehow fit.

The whole house was full of stuff just like it. His
dad loved the old farm tools and artifacts of the
early 1900's and collected them. Jack understood
his father's sentimentality and likewise collected
stuff from the 1950s and 60s. He secretly wished
he had been born a decade earlier in the 1940s and
experienced the Big Band Swing music first hand
when it was all new. He held a favorite day-dream
escape about Hot Rods and the beach scene in
Southern California.

Jack was 16 when he helped his father, George,
dismantle an old barn next to the interstate. A big
"FREE" sign the farmer had set against the falling
structure was too good of an offer for George to pass
up. It came about while heading East on I-94 after
attending a NASCAR race at Michigan International

Speedway. George made an abrupt lane change and exit off the interstate to take the frontage road to the barn. At the farm, George spoke with the farmer and examined the dilapidated structure. Then Jack and George returned the following week with a big stake bed truck George had borrowed from a friend. Crow bars in hand, father and son carefully made piles of the weathered barn siding planks and beams by measurement. Then loaded the truck and drove east to the Hamptons.

The covered piles of wood sat for a few years under tarps until George had an architect draft his idea of the perfect retirement house in the shape of a barn. The main room was built with the weathered barn wood beams and siding on the inside walls. Jack was on a ship in the US NAVY at the time of construction, so the whole place came as a surprise upon returning home. Where a small utility building once stood, was now a red barn with white trim.

In the kitchen, Jack poured a large travel mug of strong coffee, snapped on the plastic lid and walked into the living room. This is where most of the Michigan barn wood was located. At the far end of the room was an over-sized fireplace and mantle, around it were antique tools and implements. At the opposite side of the room, there was a loft and a wet bar under it. The place was full of antique farm stuff and had a museum feel with items of vastly different time periods. A Gasoline pump of the 1950's next to wagon wheel glass topped tables, lever operated water pump, a 1960s Parking meter, a 1970's traffic light, and a 1930's vintage mechanical slot machine standing around the perimeter of the bar. Old ceramic advertising signs adorned the weathered wood covered walls. In the middle of the room, a large L-shaped brown velour couch and a pair of Lazy-Boy loungers.

He set the coffee cup next to the tenor sax case sitting on the bar top. "Not this time," he whispered to the gleaming brass instrument, "too dangerous." The 1967 Selmer 6 was his best Tenor horn, but this occasion was only a "practice toot" to find the notes. Just a small splash of salt water in the seams and on the soft leather pads would mean an expensive rebuild. Jack wished he bought the plastic saxophone he saw at a music trade show. It was an interesting idea and would be an idea for today … an inexpensive alto sax to use in wet and dirty conditions. You could blow a few mellow notes while surfing, and then perhaps play a samba from the bubbling waters of a hot tub. He smiled at the thought while slipping the neoprene neck strap over his head and then scooped some #3 reeds into his pocket.

Behind the bar, hung some other musical instruments he grew up with. Among the decorative "wall hangers" … a 1940's vintage Regal Dobro guitar from his Uncle Jim … a King student trumpet from grade school band ... and a 1920's Conn C Melody Sax. He lifted the still playable old Conn sax off its hook, the mouthpiece and ligature he kept on it. Out the door, coffee cup in one hand and the antique silver plated sax in the other, he headed toward the garage.

"Baa dip datt dodily doo" ... kept repeating in his head as he grabbed a cushion, life vest and boat engine key.

Once at the dock, Jack laid the orange life vest at the bow of the boat and into the middle of it placed the old silver plated saxophone with its gold-wash bell facing back. The 14 foot aluminum boat had been his sister's but she never used it, ultimately gifting it to him a few years ago.

Moments later, the little four-stroke motor was quietly humming as he sipped the coffee and gazed back at the barn house through the fog ... assured Samantha and Argus were still asleep. After a few minutes of picking through the clutter of small boats moored on Cold Spring Pond, he found the channel to the Great Peconic Bay and a much heavier layer of fog. Barely making out the shoreline, Jack crept along by instinct and navigational memory formed since the age of seven. Having grown up plying some kind of board or boat through these waters, he mused the only difference now at 52, was all just a matter of eye-strain.

The motor quietly did its job and pushed the boat along to pass the green post marking the inlet. From here, it was just twenty-five degrees or so off to the right to dead-reckon the mid-Peconic Bay Coast Guard navigation buoy.

Jack couldn't see it, but it was there just a few miles out. The thick fog condensed into droplets on his face as he eyed the silver saxophone cushioned in the orange bundle of the life preserver.

"Baa dip datt dodily doo"

He was confident in direction but still a little surprised, yet satisfied his dead reckoning was as accurate as the dark object appeared through the fog dead ahead. The slender ghostly apparition darkened and grew into the deep red ten-foot tall buoy. He slowed the motor to approach at idle speed.

The water and sky color ran together into a flat and featureless continuum making it hard to see where the water's surface began and the atmosphere ended.

On approach to the buoy, he steered to the right and stopped the motor. It wasn't moving. The bell inside was silent. Straight up it sat, seemingly immovable, like some kind of monolith. The boat slowed to a spot just a few yards off from it.

"Slack tide", he muttered aloud, peering at the buoy's waterline, noting no little eddy swirls of a current.

Jack sipped coffee for a moment to savoir the absence of color and sound, the complete loss of sky and sea ... floating in a realm of grayness. It made him feel so calm and empty that it was easy for him to imagine what the afterlife might be like. No sound ... no objects ... just the soul floating in nothingness.

Another sip of coffee in silence and reflection ... the water was so smooth as to mirror the fog above it. Putting the cup on the floor of the boat sounded intrusively loud, like a drum. He tapped a slow 60 beat-per-minute 4/4 rhythm on the thin aluminum hull and noted how it resounded like a drum putting sound waves into the water.

This was an easy tempo for the simple musical phrase he awoke to this morning and instantly decided to use it in a little flourish at the end to one of his favorites, "Summer Time". He slipped a reed into his mouth and retrieved the sax from the orange life vest and clipped it to the strap around his neck. A moment later the tenor reed was on the C melody mouthpiece, *"You'll just have to do it this time"* he said to the miss-matched reed.

Finding no comfortable way to sit and play the

horn, Jack slowly rose to his feet. Despite the tippy nature of the little boat, he could carefully balance, tap the beat and face the big red buoy.

He blurted a few notes of the C-Scale before resetting the reed. The 1934 composition by George Gershwin, "Summer Time" was one of his favorites ... playing it softly at first, but ending with a raspy growl.

"Summertime an' the livin' is easy ...." "**Baa dip datt dodily doo**"

The song reminded him of the past ... some good times and some not ... faces of people no longer around and some of the punctuation marks their presence made in his life. Keeping the same slow tempo, "Over the Rainbow" seemed a natural second choice. The 1939 composition by Harold Arlen:

"Somewhere over the rainbow ..." And again ending with his new little phrase **"Baa dip datt dodily doo"**

ONE-QUARTER INCH

Facing "Mr. Death" for the first time … and surviving! It was the first serious consequence of a really stupid act … the outcome of choices left to deal with after the "Physicality" issue … one could either brush the whole thing off and continue merrily along as if nothing happened … or consider engaging a bit of cerebral sparkle before doing something stupid that may bring "Mr. Death" back for a visit in the future.

It would be easy say Jack was a happy kid. At seven, on a nice sunny day on Long Island, he rode with his dad to work. Jack didn't often get to be with his dad, just the two of them together. During the week, George left early to work before Jack got up and came home after he was already in bed for the night. It wasn't clear what his father did, but this particular day he would find out. George was taking Jack to New York City where he is an advertising guy at a big firm with lots of important clients. Jack was standing in the passenger foot well of the big Lincoln town car with his elbows on the dashboard. He felt really good and told his father so, but something bothered him.

"Dad, why does everything have to change?" Jack asked while staring out the window at all the other drivers going the same direction.

"Change?" he asked, "What do you mean by that?"

George looked down from above the steering wheel and their eyes met for a moment.

"Well, I'm getting older and everything is changing. Everything! And I have to change too, but I don't want to."

"Why do you say that?"

"Why can't things just stay the same without changing? I'd like to stay right here. I'm happy right now and don't want to change anything" Jack said. "I'm happy being your kid and happy with the way things are … and it all goes away with changes."

"Oh! I see what you mean," he said slowly. "I'm happy right now, too! Just the way things are. But, you will see that changes aren't so bad and may even get to like them. I just know that you are going to have a lot of changes in your life, Jack. Some may not be fun, so you have to enjoy the good ones while you can."

Jack didn't say much after that … until the elevator doors opened to his dad's fifteenth floor office.

George had a pretty secretary named Yvonne, who came right over to them to say hello. George had to talk with some other men, so Yvonne took Jack's hand and they walked to the kitchen. In the corner was a small car that was kid size! Yvonne told Jack that he could get in it and try it on "for size." The little boy was thrilled. The car didn't have pedals to pump; instead it had an electric motor. It had forward and reverse, Jack drove it around the office carpeted floor.

When Jack went into Dad's office, the window went from floor to ceiling and faced a big church across the street. Every time he got close to the window and looked down, Jack's throat tightened and felt sick. All the people walking down below were tiny. The honking taxis and busses looked like he could play with them. But his head pounded and he felt like throwing-up.

On the way home, Jack told his dad that some changes were good ... like the kid-size car and Yvonne. But that he didn't like looking out his office window. Sometime later, it was Christmas, but the kid-size car showed up at the house! He knew he liked driving. That was a change that was A-Okay!

A decade later, the family left New York and moved to Michigan and more of those "changes." It was the spring of 1969, school was out for the summer months, and Jack was literally counting the days to his 16th birthday and getting a Drivers License. It was the most important thing ... correct that, the ONLY thing that occupied his mind for every waking minute. Everybody knows that getting the license to drive is the key to having a girlfriend. No girl wants to go on a date if his mother is driving. Jack only had to use an older sister/driver a few times to realize that was just as bad ... and it would be the last and only date with that girl ... no matter how great a time they had.

While Jack's body was changing, his social skills hadn't followed. He faced a lot of girl-rejection and hadn't figured out the "information network" that all girls conspiratorially shared. He presumed it was partly because they had only moved to the neighborhood a few years earlier and he got labeled by the kids in school as a "City Slicker" from New York. Despite trying to tell the kids at the bus stop that the family didn't come from New York City, the "outsider" label stuck.

George had resisted the advertising firm's relocation attempts to move him to Michigan for many years ... until it became an ultimatum! Their biggest client, the "Tri-Motors" Car Company, wanted the top ad guy to be more accessible. George on the other hand wanted to stay out of the Corporate Office environment at "headquarters" and much preferred the independence of a Field Position ... and New York City was his oyster.

The family had lived in the highly manicured Long Island suburb of Garden City. It was a planned community in every respect. All of the streets freshly paved and shouldered by concrete curbing, setback sidewalks, bright street lights and community layout with schools, downtown, pool and shopping center all within modest walking distance.

Auburn Hills, Michigan by contrast, was a mix of classy lakefront estate property and equestrian residences with dirt roads, mailboxes, small farms and wooded areas. They moved into the former mayor's house. It was an old two-level colonial built atop a small hill in the tony horse section, about a half mile down the paved section of Squirrel Road from the Hunt Club. Stone columns marked the start of the long narrow backward-S driveway that was hidden from the street view by shrubbery that lined it. The gray two story house was old and featured a steeply pitched roof and looked down to the street below. The top of the drive curved to the left around a large enclosed porch and opened to a parking area and garage. The "gentleman farm" had pump house, chicken coop, garbage incinerator, and a little prefab insulated building that Jack's mom, Nancy, used for her dachshund breeding activities. There were three livestock stalls beneath the two car garage.

It was a typical weekend ringing phone in the kitchen that Jack answered with his usual *"Hello?"*

"Hi, this is Beth from across the street … is this Jack?" she asked.

"Uhmmm … yeah … Hi, Beth" he responded. The electricity her voice created made the hairs on the back of his neck stand up.

"Your pony is over here in our garage again."

"Oh … uhhh, okay, I'll be right over" he said and hung up.

Beth was a small and very cute girl with butt-long straight brown hair who lived two doors down the street on the opposite side. Even though they had the same school bus stop, they didn't talk much. He thought she liked him and he often found himself looking at her. She too, often caught him in a glance, and when she did, would quickly divert her eyes or attention elsewhere. Her best-friend and confidant was Cathy who lived down the street on the other side of Jack's house. Cathy had short black hair and had similar features as Beth, so he was fond of both. Beth was a little Tom-Boyish and her BFF, Cathy was a bit more girly. He couldn't decide who he liked more.

He moved quickly out the back door. The family pony, Gidget, had been breaking out and going over there with greater frequency and he needed to act quickly. Nancy's dog Lucky, a black, white and caramel colored Australian Collie mix, sensed the excitement and followed. Jack crossed the driveway toward the steps leading down to the stalls under the garage. Once there, he saw that Gidget had kicked or pushed out a horizontal plank from the outside pen. Inside the door, he picked the six foot lead off the peg at the side of a stall and started down the hill towards the stone columns out front. Lucky and Jack crossed the yard where the ram and companion sheep were grazing on the front lawn.

"Talk to her about something …. not just about Gidget," he said to himself at the edge of Squirrel Road. But that was the problem. The only thing he knew about Beth was the bus rides to school or seeing her atop a tall white quarter horse.

Lucky was not disposed to leaving the grounds and stayed near the stone columns at the base of the driveway.

"This time … say something!" he whispered to himself. *"This happens every time I get to the Grayson's house next door … brain-freeze!"*

Beth's two sisters were watching him from their front yard as he approached. They live on the outside of a banked blind corner that local drivers take way too quickly. There has been more than an occasional scare between horse, vehicle and riders.

"Hi! Is your sister around?"

The youngest girl pointed toward the driveway. Funny how the three daughters were identical copies of their mother with long straight hair, pixy nose and pointed chin. A moment later as he was nearing up their driveway, and could see at the opposite end of it an open garage door and Gidget's butt. Beth appeared at the back door of the house, *"Gidget keeps coming over here! I think we should start charging you for what she eats! Aren't you feeding her?"*

"Yes! Of course we feed her!"

"Well ... we always find her in the Omolene," she scolded, *"... and that starts Penelope whinnying, 'cause it's her Omolene."*

"Sorry about that, Beth. She kicked out another board on the pen. I'll put it back on with bigger nails this time." He said as they neared the garage, *"Do you know how long she's been here?"*

"No idea," she replied, *"Anne heard Penelope and told me, and I called you right away."*

"Well, we've started to build a coral in the backyard along the railroad tracks. It'll be pretty big. She'll be able to run around and get her exercise back there from now on."

Inside the garage, the big white horse, Penelope was agitated. Gidget had her head buried inside their metal can containing the sack of fermented malt grains busily munching away. Jack snapped the lead to the underside of Gidget's halter, led her outside and tied her to a hitching post.

"Well," Beth said looking at the sack in the can, *"... it may not be that much ... this time. But this is becoming a regular thing ..."*

He looked at the house and noticed her mother watching them from the side door. She was a bit taller than her daughter but also had long straight hair to her middle back. At a distance, they looked like sisters.

Beth looked him in the eyes and asked, *"Are you going back east for the summer?"*

"Yeah, looks like July and August and then ..."

"What?"

"I'm going to a prep school in Massachusetts this fall."

"You ... you're leaving?" her brow furrowed.

"Yea ... grades ... for college ... I'll be around though," he confessed.

"Oh!" she said with a slight pout.

"Uhmm, is your mom upset?" he asked with a slight gesture towards the house.

"Don't worry! I'll tell her that Gidget didn't eat much!"

"Oh … no sweat, I'll take her home and bring back a bucket of our Omolene to replace what she ate." He said and turned to untie Gidget.

The house side door opened. *"Beth is everything okay?"*

"Yeah, mom! Everything's okay!"

"Sorry Mrs. Young! We're making repairs now … won't happen again" he waved.

"Jack, you don't have to bring any back, it's okay" Beth said in a low voice.

"Oh? … Uhmm … well … ahhh …" he stammered, trying to think of something else to talk about, *"I'll be seeing you around. Thanks!"*

He led Gidget down the driveway. He looked back over his shoulder, but Beth and her sisters were gone.

On their way past the Grayson's house, Jack strained to see if the Triumph motorcycle was still there. Charlie and his sister Sarah lived there. They were another two kids at the bus stop. Jack and his younger brother, Calvin didn't hang with them much, especially after Jack re-assembled the Triumph 500 Speed Twin. Their dad, a criminal attorney, had a client go to prison and all that was left to collect afterwards, a disassembled motorcycle. Some months past, Jack had to retrieve Calvin who was over at their house and their dad asked if Jack could put it back together. Jack said he could, and took all the stuff home. He cleaned, painted and reassembled it. Then jump wired with the tractor battery and got it running, too. When he took it back to their house, all he heard was a *"Thanks! Now I can get my money out of it."* He didn't offer a dime for the effort and Jack never went back.

"Cheap Ass!" he muttered walking past.

Further up Squirrel, just to the north and across the street were the Joneses. Cathy Jones often sat with Beth at the front of the school bus. Last Halloween's Devil's Night, Cathy and Jack walked up the road past Beth's house as they headed south on Squirrel to the Sacred Heart school. There in the front of the school stood an eight foot tall statue of the Mother Mary with outstretched arms ... the two trouble makers toilet-papered the statue to look like a ghost. Cathy sat on Jack's shoulders to reach the upper parts, and did most of the decorating, on top of him long enough to get an erection. Thanks to it being a dark night, he was spared the embarrassing presence of his swollen member. Then he remembered the famous line from an old Mae West movie, "Is that a pistol in your pocket or are you just really glad to see me?" Jack was ready to blurt out "It's a pistol!", but didn't have to use it.

The next day, the kids on the bus erupted as it rode past the ghost on the lawn. They both felt guilty for desecrating a holy thing ... and never talked about it afterwards.

The family dog, Lucky was still sitting at the end of the driveway by the stone columns when Jack returned with Gidget. He happily followed Jack and the pony back to the stalls under the garage. Jack grabbed the hammer left down there with a can of 2" common nails. A few minutes later, the fence was fixed ... until the next time Gidget felt compelled to break out.

He grabbed the shovel and hoe, then, went to work cleaning up the pony doo-doo in Gidget's stall. They kept the small tractor and trailer in the stall area under the garage these days. Every few weeks, Jack's younger brother Calvin and he had to scoop all the muck in the stall/outside pen area and dump the manure out in back next to the railroad tracks.

The tractor and trailer that were used to move the poop was kept in one of the stalls. The upper level garage was full of antique car parts, the result of George going to a Chicago antique car auction/flea market and making a "good deal." The rental truck he drove back had enough parts to build two complete cars ... it became Jack's assignment to make one "good" one from them.

Lucky was a happy dog and loved the herding part he played on the grounds. He hung around the back door of the house as he made himself available on a moment's notice to round up the chickens, the ram and his harem of sheep. Yes, things were very different here than Garden City, New York. In addition to the feeding, watering and cleanup activities, Jack became skilled at the basics of hoof maintenance, and sheep shearing.

Lucky and Jack ran up the side yard steps to the driveway. As usual, several dachshunds of the dozen or so, made a cacophony of barking anytime anyone was present.

Nancy had a hobby/business of breeding and showing them. She operated out of a small one-room building at the peak of the little hill about half-way to the rear of the property. While there were outdoor dog runs up there, she often kept some portable pens around the driveway area, and these were always occupied with arrivals and departures of dachshunds for breeding, boarding or for an occasional sale. All of the dogs, except Lucky, were shuttled every day from the basement in the house to one of the penned areas outside then back to the basement again to spend the night. This was typically a big effort in cleanup and each dog was identified for a specific location, feeding and breeding regimen. Several times a day, the commuter trains could be heard in the distance and give a short whistle on approach to the station, just a quarter mile away. So Nancy named her kennel "Whistle Station Farm".

George had ordered the boards and posts for the corral they were going to build, be dropped-off by the lumber yard, at the base of the driveway. Calvin and Jack used the tractor and trailer to move all the material from the foot of the driveway up and over the hill to the back area in the depression next to the tracks. Although it was still a little early for the big Michigan mosquitoes to swarm, the pesty little biters showed no mercy and required the strongest of repellants. The area for most of the corral was low and boggy. George thought the lowest area could be flat-blade plowed by the tractor to create a pond. It didn't work as the whole thing turned into a mud hole, which the mosquitoes liked even more.

Saturday morning, George rented a gas powered auger to drill the post holes. With a guide string running from one corner of the coral to the next, the post holes for the entire coral were bored in just a few hours. Then each post bottom was painted with tar, dropped into a hole, leveled, boarded and backfilled. The backfill job was an easy one since all the dirt surrounded each hole.

By late afternoon at almost quitting time, Calvin and Jack swapped driving the tractor and trailer around transporting tools, tar and poles. The auger machine went to the upper garage for return to the rental center; all the other stuff with the tractor and trailer went to the lower garage, where the stalls were located.

As usual, Gidget was tethered to a stake in the ground in the front yard. Butch and sheep were loose as they hung around and rarely left the grounds. Every so often, Gidget had to be moved otherwise, there would have been a perfect circle in the grass around wherever she was staked. Calvin went off to move her. George went to the stalls. And Jack took the tractor for a final sweep of tools or anything left out back.

Driving ... the nearness of the Driver's License was an intoxicating thought. Someday, he daydreamed that he'd even drive a race car. The little blue tractor became his "practice" race car that could whizz around the yard like a go-kart.

Jack was fairly certain that there weren't tools overlooked and left lying on the ground, but he didn't need much of an excuse to hop on the tractor for a spin. Down in the lower area of the coral where George's recent "pond" excavation bared the loamy soil, the tractor's fat little tires spun and kicked up dirt. Like an off-road racer, he jumped the excavation berms and got into awesome sideways slides with the tires spinning and spitting dirt. Two laps around the coral, no tools were visible and so the racing tractor had to go to the pits.

Climbing up the steep hill, he slipped the tractors clutch to slowly steer through the line of post holes and once clear, popped it to get some more wheel spin. But the tires dug in and the front of the tractor lifted straight up and over on top of him …. In an instant, the steering wheel was next to his face and "CRUNCH!"

He crawled out from under the tractor and turned it off. *"Damn!"* he said as he sat on the ground, *"Dad's gonna be pissed!"*

Jack couldn't focus. The left side of his head felt numb. He closed his left eye and looked at the tractor resting upside down. With a heave, he turned it over back onto its tires … the hood was scraped and the steering wheel flattened. He still couldn't focus and noticed the blood on his white t-shirt. He franticly pulled on the steering wheel to make it look normal ... no good.

Ringing in his ears grew really loud as he walked back to the house. He heard Nancy talking to someone on the kitchen phone as he headed to the small bath next to George's study. The face in the mirror was a blur of mud and blood. The wet wash cloth helped to cool the left side burn that was increasing. He braced himself on the vanity and looked into the mirror again. Lowering the wash cloth from his face ... *"Oh, shit!"* he whispered, *"No girl is gonna want this! I'm screwed!"* His left cheekbone was gone and his sideburn now protruded wide enough to hide his left ear.

"Wait! Wait!" he coached himself to rinse the wash cloth out and dab his face a little more. The wet cloth soothed the burn. Jack lowered the cloth again as he looked with both eyes ... still couldn't focus, but the face was still hideous. *"I'm NEVER going to EVER get a girlfriend now!"*

He walked into the kitchen. Nancy was off the phone and writing something on her calendar.

"Uhh ... Mom?"

"Yes, dear, what?" she said without looking up.

"I've got a little problem."

She looked up. He removed the wash cloth.

"OH MY GOD! OH MY GOD!" she jumped and ran to the back door.

"I had a little accident with the tractor ..."

"GEORGE! GEORGE!" she called, *"Oh, my god!"*

Jack heard his father's voice in the distance and the ensuing urgent words to take him to an Emergency Room.

Burning pain masked the flurry of what followed, as Jack was hustled into the station wagon and driven to Pontiac Hospital. Emergency Room staff put him on a gurney ... nurses and doctors came and went ... waiting and pain. The medical staff ascertained his stability for a longer wait as other patients were admitted with more urgent life-saving procedures. They wouldn't release him to be driven to the Henry Memorial Hospital by his parents, so he was rolled out to a hallway and awaited an ambulance transfer. It seemed like hours ...

Awakening in a different place, someone said Jack had already been through OR and his folks were here. Everything was morphine fuzzy. Nancy, George and a doctor were there. The doctor was holding a little flashlight to his face as he described the operation.

"We built up the maxilla here … and the mandible here … wired them into place. Fortunately, we could do this from this incision under his eye and over here, next to the ear," he said as the little flashlight criss-crossed Jack's face. *"How are you doing, Jack?"*

"Okay" he responded, *"but it hurts!"*

"We're going to give you something for the pain, Jack, in just a few more minutes, Okay?"

"Okay."

The doctor mumbled something to the nurse, and then continued waving his little flashlight around. *"So, I'll have some more tests and x-rays done tomorrow, we'll have him go through Neurology, Optometry, Dental, … and ahhh, Auditory testing just to be sure. But I think we're in good shape … just a quarter inch more in any direction, you see … "* he continued moving the light about to emphasize, *"… for sure there'd be a loss of vision … or hearing … or teeth … and over this way it could have been fatal."*

The days that followed were a morphine haze and although he was home within a week, he never spoke with Beth Young again. Until his lumpy face healed some more, Jack was afraid of her reaction upon seeing it. Rejection by the female gender was hard for him to take. It was an inauspicious beginning to his second life.

Jack's public High School grades were too low for gaining College admission. His parents had already made the decision that a private ivy-league style preparatory school was the answer. A few weeks later, he got packed off to a mid state Massachusetts all-male preparatory school.

KANSAS CITY SLIDER

Freshman year at Denton University was a bust. Situated in the rolling hills east of Columbus, Ohio in the small community of Grainfield, the campus had that "Ivy League" New England look and feel. Similar to the Winndon School from which Jack had just graduated. Actually, it seemed that the only difference was the availability of alcohol, marijuana ... and female students. Although Grainfield was a "dry" town which had neither a bar nor allowed adult-beverage retail sales, the nearby town of Newmark, about 6 miles away, had plenty. On the other hand, cheap pot was everywhere on campus.

Incoming freshmen were prohibited from having a vehicle. It meant the only beer that they could get their hands on was the 3.2% alcohol that was served at campus social events. Getting home to Auburn Hills was a 3-hour drive north through Toledo to Detroit and most of the time, meant cold and wet conditions. So dormitory life was a behavioral mess ... kids away from the influence of their parents for the first time in their lives ... most of them from the mid-west ... packed into the same dorms together ... the chance of having a good roommate was slim. It was only two weeks into the semester when the musical roommate game got started ... just like the kid parlor game of musical chairs, partner swaps led to other partner swaps. He had four different roommates in the first semester. Added on top of that was the "Pre-Med" curricula of heavy lab-oriented sciences ... not good.

"Pre-Med" was Nancy's idea. "My son ... the Doctor!" she would say. Perhaps it was the repetition, or the gratitude he felt after having his tractor smashed face repaired. After awhile, he thought "why not?" Doctors made good dough ... helped people ... were respected in society ... blah, blah, blah. So he'd give it a try.

Needless to say, he bombed his GPA from the very start and kissed good-bye any hopes of moving on to a medical career. English Literature sounded like a good second choice for a major.

Second semester was only slightly better. Still campus bound with no transportation, when a Harley Davidson motorcycle hit the bulletin board for $450, he couldn't resist! It was a 1948 Panhead 74 c.i. Full Dresser Touring model, all original with springer front fork, crash bars, windshield, saddle bags, foot clutch – hand shifter, dual gas tanks, big wheels, tires and fender trim. The guy whom

Jack contacted said that it was being sold for a student who already left the campus and that it was in a fraternity house basement. The idea of mobility was the motivator, but that all went out the window once he saw it. The Peter Fonda and Dennis Hopper movie, Easy Rider, prompted him to do the logical thing and build a "chopper" outlaw custom bike.

So he promptly took it all apart and moved it into the dorm room. Because of its tight space, he tossed all the parts he wouldn't need except for the engine, frame and rear wheel. Over the period of a few months, it was finished but virtually un-ride able. The peanut size fuel tank was only good for 60 to 75 miles, it didn't have a speedometer, any turn signals or front brake, rode hard on the butt without any rear suspension, and he couldn't carry anything.

After the semester ended, it went home to Auburn. He rode it around awhile before the family planned summer break in the Hamptons. He got George's agreement to ride it to Long Island. He followed in the station wagon behind Jack on the bike. By the time Jack got to Detroit via Interstate 75, the engine died from fuel starvation. George dutifully pulled behind him. Jack took out a gas can in the back of the car and refilled the Harley's tiny tank. He didn't notice that he pulled off the rubber fuel line from the tank which doused the engine in gasoline ... needless to say, the bike erupted in flames!

Jack switched off the fuel petcock at the base of the tank and stopped the flow of gas. But he hopped about trying to put the flames out. A trailer-less big rig pulled over, the driver casually pulled out a fire extinguisher and sauntered over, looked at the bike and then gave it a puff of foam. It killed the flames and covered the bike in creamy goo. Jack thanked the driver who didn't say anything, slowly turned to face his tractor rig and sauntered back.

Realizing it was a long way to New York, travel would be slow with frequent fuel stops, and uncertain mechanical issues that awaited the expedition. George saw the disappointment in Jack's face as he said they'd have to take it back to Auburn. George offered to throw it into the station wagon for the trip duration. Jack didn't want to remove the long front fork on it because of all the greased ball bearings that would spill out on the side of the road. So, instead they put the ass-end into the wagon with the front wheel almost touching the pavement, drove it back home and left it in the garage.

The trip to New York was faster, far less painful, and Jack was pretty quiet. George sensed that Jack was really bummed about it all and didn't say much.

A few days of running around the beaches really helped. Jack was surprised when George gave him a car almost one month before his birthday. It was a special car. George had bought the Fairlane Victoria new in 1955 as a gift to his parents for their 45th Wedding Anniversary. Since then, George's father passed, his mother didn't drive and that Fairlane just sat in the single stall garage behind his parents' house for 16 years. With very little mileage it was almost new. The interior bench seats were protected with clear plastic covers, like the ones they kept on their couches and chairs in their house. All that it needed was a set of fresh tires and it was ready to go.

It had a two-tone paint scheme of rose/beige over white, 4 doors, 272 cubic inch V-8 engine with a three-on-the-tree shifter. The trunk was big and the front and rear seats could sit three people across. Jack wasted no time in removing those clear plastic seat covers as one's legs got singed after heating up in the summer sun. Big beach towels to cover the bench seats were more comfortable and visually appealing.

Back in Auburn, Jack wasted no time in selling the Harley just before heading off to campus and the first sophomore semester full of potential!

Sophomore girls seemed friendlier and he thought he was beginning to figure out that he was too easy to read. He must have been telegraphing his romantic intentions. He didn't catch-on to the visual process of females ... they had to watch you awhile first. It wasn't until Jack observed some girls chatting amongst themselves and covertly taking glances at every new guy arriving and then analyzing his moves. Even Jack could guess who got shot down! Looks didn't seem to matter. If he stepped in, scanned his prey and approached it was the first "strike." His target was the next evaluation. If it happened to be the hottest girl(s), "strike two." If the conversation starting line he used was lame, "strike three."

Arrive early, hang out, be observant, suppress any feelings of attraction and pretend only to be seeking "fun."

Jack was now residing at the opposite end of campus on the 2nd floor of Crandall Hall with a very smart roommate named Ralph. Actually, he was too smart and didn't have to study to get great grades, so he was always ready to party ... and often was!

The dorm was huge and housed 600 male students, two to a room, three floors high. Theirs was on the second floor situated next to a stairwell with a view of a large outside courtyard and parking lot. Not that the view mattered, the window got covered with a thick blanket to darken the room, but just enough daylight to give the room a low-glow at noon.

Anyway, the Fairlane took Jack everywhere ... to hiking and camping at Hocking Hills State Park ... to the trails climbing the water falls of Old Man's Cave ... and getting high. The one thing Jack knew how to do was drive safely with any passengers. Soon, he had many Detroit area girls looking for a holiday ride to and from campus in exchange for a little gas money. What could be better? He had full loads of five girls for the three hour drive ... and cute ones at that! He always ended up with a few dollars after buying gas. Life was good!

In early December, classes were about to end. Most students had one week before an onslaught of final exams at mid-month ... just before going home for the Christmas Holidays.

Jack's roommate, Ralph, appeared to be asleep when there was a knock at the door. Still bleary-eyed and wearing only a pair of jeans, he reluctantly interrupted his sock search to open it. It was Tim and Joe, his best friends. A collection of contrasts, Tim was medium build, long blonde hair like a lion's mane, and had an air of nervousness about him. Joe, on the other hand, had a slight build with black straight "Dutch Boy" hair, appearing emotionless with a monk-like serenity.

"Hey, man … it's time to get up!" said Tim and took a drag on his cigarette.

"You're missing a beautiful day!" Joe added.

Suddenly, the voice behind him, *"Yeah man, let's rally!"*

"Alright!" Tim said stepping into the darkness of the room, *"that's more like it!"*

Catapulting out of bed, Ralph pulled back the curtain to flood the room with sunshine and blue sky. He opened the window and leaned out of it to empty the smelly bong liquid. He was tall, stout and big framed with a small Roman nose and brown wavey shoulder length hair surrounding a round face with oversized mutton-chop sideburns. Wearing the small oval wire framed glasses; Ralph looked a bit like an old-timey founding fathers politician like you'd see in a history book photo. *"I'll get it together, man"* he said, pulling on his brown led zeppelin concert t-shirt

"So you guys all studied up for exam week?" asked Joe.

"No, not really," Jack said *"I've got a lot of back reading to do … wasted too much time and didn't do much reading."*

"I'll put on some tunes" said Ralph as he walked

over to the stereo reel-to-reel tape machine, studied the counter and backed up the tapes to a specific spot. Then he turned on the quadraphonic stereo that had speakers in each corner of the room simulating surround sound. "Thump thump thump thump!" the heart beat rhythm at the beginning of the Pink Floyd dark side of the Moon album, was Ralph's latest acquisition and his favorite.

"Man, I got a lot of economics to read up on" Tim said, *"And ... with finals coming up in a week. Man, I gotta do something about my shitty GPA."*

"What are you talking about?" asked Ralph, *"Your grades are almost as good as mine."*

Joe sat at Jack's desk to cut up some grass to roll a joint. *"I talked to a friend this morning ... he connected me with a friend's brother in Denver who is sitting on a lot of Acapulco or Panama pot ... really good stuff and it's cheap!"*

"I have no wheels, man ... I'd do it," said Tim.

"Uhh ... do what?" Jack asked.

"Drive to Denver and bring back a couple keys of primo pot" Tim responded.

"With what?" Jack said rubbing the fingers of his right hand with the thumb to mean money.

*"That ... "*said Joe, licking the rolling paper glue to complete the roll *"...is the good part. He'll front it to me ... we can sell it on campus before Winter Break ... really good pot hasn't been around this campus in awhile ... everybody wants to take home something for the Holidays ... it would sell out really fast ... we would make some money and have a stash, too."*

"Hmmm!" Jack scratched his chin whiskers in open ponder, *"Might be something to think about!"*

Joe lit the joint and handed it off to Jack, who took a deep cough-inducing drag, then passed the joint to Tim. They listened to Pink Floyd for a bit as they smoked-n-passed it around and around.

"The only way it would work is to get that here in just a few days," Jack said with some skepticism.

"It's a straight run out there and back," Tim said, *"All of it on I-70."*

Ralph got up and left the room with his bong and a water bottle, headed for the hallway water fountain. When he got back with it refilled, said *"I could do some driving."*

The three of them looked at each other, then at Jack, the only one with a reliable car. Joe's beat-up black Mustang barely got him to and from

Pittsburgh only 150 miles away. The Denver trip is 1,300 miles each way.

"Yeah, man," Jack said "But, I don't have enough gas money to get there and back."

"We can scratch that up," Joe said, "The whole thing has to be done fast … like leave right now … drive for two days … get the stuff … drive back for two days … the sooner, the better."

As if by magic, Floyd's 'Money' played. Jack contemplated the adventurous road trip with its benefits.

"I'm pretty sure he could front two kilos and that would be 70 one-ounce bags. We sell an ounce of primo for fifty-bucks … that's $3,500 … double the cost to get it" Joe reasoned, "Primo pot! … and some Christmas money!"

"I'll go with you, man" Ralph said to Jack, "we can team drive and not stop. I don't have to worry about the school stuff … got that covered."

"Alternate driving and sleeping in the back seat …" Jack murmured, "Hmmmm!" Jack scratched his chin again. "Ehhh … I suppose … "

"Bring back as much Coors beer as the car will hold and … that's even better!" Tim suggested. Jack had to admit, Coors beer was only available in Colorado and highly valued back here. Like the popular Jack Denver song, who wouldn't want to get "Rocky Mountain High?"

Ralph's bong kept getting reloaded and passed around and Jack was getting blasted.

The munchies were hitting him now. *"I need to hit up the cafeteria before it closes,"* he said. *"If I'm going to drive ... I need to stop smoking and get food."*

They left the dorm and made it to the cafeteria before it closed out the lunch service period. Over lunch, the map was viewed, distance and time added, mileage and fuel calculated, and finally, the amount of money they needed. It was all do-able and they had to act fast. Jack tossed some underwear, socks, t-shirt and a toothbrush into a bag and then took a nap to clear up the pot head and rest for the nights driving stint.

They departed just before 6 pm that night; cash in hand, directions, travel change and full tank of fuel. Jack was taking the first driving stint. It was going to be Interstate 70 West all the way there. Ralph was too wired up to sleep and so he rode in the front seat during the first part. That is, he sat there until the flashing red and blue lights filled the rear view mirrors. The Indiana Trooper stopped them for driving with only one working headlight. Jack exited the Fairlane and walked to the front with the Trooper, while his partner flashed his light around the car's interior and Ralph. Yep, the headlight out, Jack banged on it with his fist and it flickered and went back on. The Trooper let them go with a verbal warning to get it fixed so that it stays on.

"I meant to ask you. How did it go with the cheerleader the other night? You guys were getting pretty cozy at the bar."

"It was a no-go," Ralph said. *"Hotties can be a problem. Decided not to go there."*

"Really? She was so fucking hot. I thought you'd want to tap that."

"I'm telling you, I've dated a lot of girls," Ralph said,*"... all different kinds. They all fall into one of two types, Hotties or Tomboys."*

"Hotties or Tomboys?"

"Yeah. The Hotties are visually attractive, gorgeous even. These narcissistic girls know what their assets are and how to exploit them. They spend all their time trying to find stuff to create a new look for themselves that's even more attractive. Call it a study in packaging and marketing! You know ... girly-girls. They try to attract every guy by how they

dress, jewelry, makeup, hair and strut about. But once you fuck 'em, you realize that there's nothing to talk about. Tastes great, less filling"

"Gee, that's dark," Jack countered. *"So, every pretty girl is a narcissist?"*

"Just calling 'em how I see 'em."

Jack didn't say anything.

Then Ralph continued, *"It depends on the level of detail they put into appearance. A hottie can talk about safe topics like travel, food, style and pets or children without appearing narcissistic. And every guy thinks about giving her children. As a type, I consider the narcissistic element as a highly probable defect."*

"So you've banged a couple of cute ones and afterwards, they only wanted to go out shop for shoes and get their nails done?"

"That's my story and I'm sticking to it. It's that whole ... Women are from Venus and men are from Mars, thing."

"I may have visited Venus a few times! So what's the other type of female? The tomboys?"

Ralph was on a roll, *"Okay, Mars man. The other*

kind of chick is Tomboy. They're masculine in thinking and behavior and can make friends easily with other guys. You can go camping, fishing, ride dirt bikes, throw a ball around, go to a game ... whatever. They have an interest in doing things and don't freak-out if its grubby. Not afraid of bugs or getting dirt on themselves. These girls wanna have some fun. But they are hard to get romantic with ... you know, put out and some are dykes ... and because they make guy friends so easily ... there's that jealousy thing you gotta deal with".

"I understand your observations, but those types are extremes. I think most females don't see themselves like that, and are a little bit of both. Turn it around ... are the guy types either musculine jocks or skinny nerds?

"Walk around campus man, that's mostly what I see ... athletes and nerds!"

Jack had to kill this nonsense. *"Well I don't agree. I've had girlfriends who weren't hotties or tomboys. I just take them as they are and don't think about labels."*

They made a stop for fuel and coffee ... then he was set for the night. Ralph climbed into the back of the car and stretched out across the bench seat. Jack turned on the AM radio and listened for news and weather.

He had to make another stop at about midnight. Ralph and Jack swapped positions. Like a baby, the cars motion put him instantly to sleep.

It was almost 6 AM when Jack woke. He sat up and noticed a fair amount of snow blanketing the fields adjacent to the interstate. *"Morning, man, How are we doing?"*

"Hey, man … we're doing good. The Missouri border is just ahead and Kansas City. Sleep okay?"

"Like a rock," Jack said. *"Do you want to pull over and swap places?"*

"No, man, I'm okay for a bit, maybe after Kansas City."

"Snowed, huh?"

"Yeah. I could see okay … didn't come down that heavy. That headlight keeps blinking on and off …"

"Somewhere ahead, I will clean up the bulb contacts. No rush now."

An orange sign advised of the construction zone and I-70 detour just ahead. Another few miles and they were on the outskirts of Kansas City. The roadway elevated to form a tri-level cloverleaf with them climbing to the top. They saw the half covered orange detour sign pointing to the left ramp on the approach to the crest of the cloverleaf.

Ralph turned the steering wheel to the left, but the old Fairlane continued straight. In an instant, it was clear they weren't going to make the turn.

"FUCK! … FUCK! … FUCK!"

The Fairlane went straight up the ice pack. Jack dove behind the front bench seat and braced himself against it …. he waited for what inevitably would be the secondary impact of the car hitting the pavement the next level down … but it was silent. He heard about time stopping in moments like this … suddenly everything in slow-motion and the grim reaper is standing by the roadside waving.

But nothing happened … no second impact. He could hear Ralph ranting … all doors of the Fairlane had sprung open and it was suddenly very cold.

Jack popped his head up. The car stopped on the ramp and other traffic exiting onto the ramp slowed down to get a good look as they passed.

"What the Fuck! What happened?" Jack asked.

"You're … ALIVE!" he stammered, *"I thought for sure that you went over the railing when the doors popped open."*

Looking back at the exit ramp, one could see how the car slid up the ice-packed railing and slid along the top of the dented tubular guardrail. Somehow, call it "divine intervention", the car had balanced on the railing and didn't go over. The other side of the guardrail was a 100-foot drop with another elevated ramp below and above a ground-level street. There in the very bottom street laid Jack's duffel bag that shot out the opened door. It contained toiletries, underwear, socks and a couple of t-shirts. He looked up and down their elevated position trying to figure out which way to go to retrieve it, when a truck ran it over.

"Ah, Rats!" Jack exclaimed.

Ralph came to the guardrail, and peered down. *"Oh Fuck-me! We are sooo lucky!"*

Jack pulled a pipe out of his pocket. Ralph saw him toss it off the overpass. Without a word, they emptied their pockets of pot, papers, lighter and everything else they didn't want to have on them as a cop would soon show up.

After impact, the car had come back off the rail onto the exit ramp. It sat cockeyed with the right front bent down and left rear sticking up, all the doors were open, the lights and left blinker still on. The right front tire was flat. Even if he replaced it with the spare, they couldn't drive it anywhere. The engine was noisy and the four doors wouldn't stay closed. There was nothing to do but wait.

Sure enough, a Kansas City squad car pulled up, lights going. Ralph faced Jack and said, *"I'm really sorry, man."* He read Jack's eyes and pulled the red and gold Russian hammer/sickle medallion off the lapel of his black woolen trench coat before the squad car door opened. He shoved it into his pocket just as the huge black officer emerged and slipped on his hat. As the officer approached, Jack marveled that this was the biggest man he had ever seen! He had to be 6 foot 6 inches and 300 pounds of body-builder muscle.

When the cop turned toward the squad car with Jack's registration and Ralph's license, the Russian star medallion went over the rail. *"Good move,"* Jack commented, *"he's probably a veteran, too."*

A few moments later, the wrecker left with the Fairlane headed for a local car dealer.

"Sorry I have to do this," the officer said to Ralph as he slipped on the handcuffs, *"The rule is that if you damage public property, I have to place you under arrest and take you in. And that guardrail is definitely damaged."*

Jack didn't get cuffs but sat next to Ralph in the back of the squad car for the ride to the station.

The snow was coming down much heavier and swirling as they made their way to the station. The officer explained to Ralph that he would be booked and that bail would be set to ensure his return for facing the judge or forfeiting the bail as a fine. Somewhat apologetically, the officer said that he'd talk this over with his supervisor and see what he could do under the circumstances.

Once in the station, Ralph got processed before he got his "free phone call". Ralph's father was pleasantly surprised to get the *"Hi dad! Uh, I've got a little problem, I was driving my friend's car and we slid off the road and I got arrested for denting the guardrail. Could you wire $300 bail? Oh, and my buddy's car is wrecked so I'll need a little more as I have no way to get back to campus ... from Kansas City!"*

Hearing a rather loud "WHAT THE HELL ARE YOU DOING IN KANSAS CITY?" coming from the telephone handset, made Ralph cringe. It triggered Jack to think about how he'll describe this predicament to George.

In the blending of Ralph's words and his dad's this had Jack thinking how he'd call his dad with a believable and yet forgivable story.

The arresting officer returned and said that he talked his supervisor out of filing the booking papers and that the charges were dropped and they were free to go! From the payphone in the station lobby, Ralph called his father back, reverse charges. It went well; his dad had settled down and wanted to talk with Jack. Ralph handed Jack the phone and his dad asked him if he had already picked out a replacement car and that he'd wire $1,500 or $1,800 to the dealer. Jack responded that they were still at the station and no, he hadn't considered another car yet. Ralph talked to his dad a bit more and said they'd call again. He hung up the phone and looked at Jack. He shook his head "NO WAY". He was glad to be alive and there was just no way they could buy a car and finish the mission to Denver, they had already lost too much time. It seemed that suddenly the path forward was clear … get back to campus, study for exams, then go home for the holidays and face the music.

Jack collect called George at his company office. *"Hi, Dad! …"* Jack's version went a bit smoother than he expected. The storyline was that they were headed out to Denver to catch a little skiing and crack the books for finals. His roomy was driving. The Fairlane got towed to the dealership. They just needed to get back to school. George was very cool about it, maybe thinking it could be repaired. He said an agency rep would come get them at the police station and take them to the airport. They would have two tickets at Will Call to get them back to Columbus.

Joe and Tim met them at the Columbus airport for the trip back to campus in Joe's junky flat black spray can painted Mustang. Needless to say, Ralph and Jack had a very animated story to tell them as they went back to Crandall Hall. No Pot ... No Coors ... Gas Money about gone ... and his girl shuttling business was bust.

The dealer examined the Fairlane and declared it a total loss ... the frame was twisted and engine block was cracked.

After the holidays, Ralph's dad reneged on replacing the car. Instead, Jack was handed a small check that covered little more than the plane fare back to Columbus. He grudgingly accepted it. The relationship between them was done even though they endured the life-threatening experience which, at the time, was a bond. The tolerance lasted until the mid-March Spring Break.

Upon returning after the Break, all of Ralph's stuff was cleared out of the dorm room they shared. Jack made nothing of it and figured he got swapped for someone else to room share. It was later that afternoon; Jack saw Joe and Tim at the Student Union and learned that Ralph suffered a fatal car crash.

This was the second time Jack could have/should have been killed by his own stupidity.

Never let someone talk you into doing something you ordinarily wouldn't and for his grand gesture, Jack lost a car. Once again, no wheels meant no dates ... Jack didn't even try.

What money Jack could save going into the last two years, bought a 1956 Porsche 356 coupe in "beater" condition. Learning how to keep it running became an ongoing study in automotive engineering that never seemed to end.

The summer was spent bouncing between New York and Detroit helping George with dismantling and transporting barn wood. George did show him a few things. As a depression-era kid, George saved everything. The garage was full of broken mechanical things, construction materials and partial paint cans. He couldn't bring himself to toss anything. Jack helped him "fix" things with the remnant stuff on hand. Cutting a piece of wood, straightening bent nails from a rusty coffee can, covering it with left-over paint, repaired something at no cost. For all his resourcefulness though, George didn't have or know how to use the proper tools for a given job. A screwdriver was a paint can opener, a pry bar, a chisel, and occasionally, putting in or removing screws.

Like God fixing the broken souls in Purgatory, George hammered things straight and repurposed them to a useful end.

TUSKER

It was May 1975, just moments after the Denton University Commencement ceremony; the Springer family stood in the crowded parking lot of the university's gymnasium. Nancy and George Springer had roped Jack's older sister, Lisa and younger brother Calvin, to attend. With the diploma in hand, all Jack wanted to do was to get out of there. The gathering was just the meeting area for newly minted graduates to connect with their families. Pictures were taken, addresses and phone numbers exchanged, farewells expressed. Nancy looked at George said something about not wanting to take the trip and why doesn't he take Jack instead. There was an International Advertising Professionals Association (IAPA) convention in Africa next week and Nancy didn't want do the trip ... not wanting to leave all her dogs for 10 days and the prospect of George being out of the house that long was like a vacation for her.

At 56, George was glad to see his son reach this milestone and hopefully, into a good job and out of the nest. Kids are expensive, especially as they enter adulthood and soon, he'll only have Calvin, the youngest to go. It's not that he relished his work at the big office, but he wasn't clamoring for retirement either.

As he gazed upon his long haired orange bearded son that George realized they were like strangers. And Jack, thought likewise. The tall man sporting a balding head and puffy white muttonchops was also a mystery despite the six years Jack was already out of the house and only an occasional holiday visitor.

"Your Mother and I are taking a trip next week and wondered if you'd like to go instead", he asked, "an African safari of sorts."

"Gee!" Jack choked, "you don't want to go, Mom?"

"No, Jack you take it and go with your Father. A few months ago, he told me about it and I said 'sure.' But I have a lot to do and it would be better if you went instead" she said.

"Heck, yeah, I'll go!"

Although Jack did not have a Passport, George had connections in New York City to expedite getting one. Jack flew to New York and was escorted through the process of a photograph, a few immunization shots and an Embassy visit for a visa.

The requirements were met for a ticketing name change and Jack was ready to go. A few days later, George would show up and they'd leave from JFK Airport together.

With an hour until boarding the Braniff plane, they sat at a bar next to the gate.

"Cheers!" the proud father said as they clinked beer glasses.

"Wow, Dad, I don't know where we're headed or what we're gonna do there, but … Thanks!"

"We are landing in London for an overnight while the rest of our group arrives. They are coming from all over. Advertising Professionals who belong to the IAPSA. We are all Advertising or APSA (Advertising Professionals Society of America) practitioners who are also IAPSA members," he said. *"I like to keep a fishing line in the international side of things … just to keep it interesting."*

He took a swig of beer and continued, *"Then we'll all go as a group to Nairobi, Kenya to the first All Africa Advertising Professionals Society Convention. They are in the beginning stages of forming a Charter for their organization and invited us to attend and provide some guidance. And add a little credibility to what they are trying to do for the continent. It's all about fostering a positive image for Africa as a place to do business and to increase tourism. And we're going to do some of that as well."*

"You mean a safari?"

"Yeah, something like that, only we will hit some of the highlights and not get into the camping kinds of thing."

The flight to London's Heathrow Airport was unremarkable. Jack was entertained by the parade of pretty stewardesses in mini-skirt outfits that kept changing during the flight. The interior of the aircraft was done in a Peter Maxx kind of Mod style matching the stewardess's attire. They all made outfit changes based on which part of the flight they were in … boarding … cocktail hour … meal hour … movie hours … and departure preparation. He almost didn't want to leave the plane! The taxi ride to the hotel was alarming. The road transportation was backward … driving on the left took getting used to even as a passenger. They checked into the Grosvener House Hotel in London, an upscale older hotel full of marble and wood paneling. George recognized a face or two from the group, but because of the time change, bypassed the impromptu "meet and greet" drinking at the bar.

The next day was full of introductions, handshakes,

and names Jack had instantly forgotten as they navigated back to the airport and boarded the flight to Kenya. Planted right on the Equator, he was prepared for hot weather with mostly shorts and t-shirts, but also brought a sport coat and tie.

In the group of about sixteen people, three of them were in their twenties and everyone else was older than fifty. The odds were in his favor! Of the three girls, the homely one, Jan, was working on a Master's Degree in Blah-blah-blah and brought her textbooks on the subject and expected to keep her nose in them. The other two, Marilyn and Vanessa, were sisters and real lookers. These two were well practiced in their male attraction skills of visual packaging and movement fluidity. Exuding the talent to exploit their physical attributes in dress, hair styling and makeup in catching men's eyes and the demure motions like sway-walking, sitting and crossing legs that keep those male eyes riveted in place. This situation commanded further investigation!

The classy little Norfolk Hotel on the main thoroughfare in downtown Nairobi had the clinging residue of British Colonialism. It featured quaint little cottages connected by winding footpaths through lush flowering fauna, the source of the heavy sweet aroma made stronger by shade and humidity. A small swimming pool with diving board and outdoor bar was located at one end of the hotel and a patio of café tables at the other end shaded by umbrellas. Once their baggage made it to their cottage, George was all for getting something to eat at the café.

"Oh boy!" George said as he studied the menu, "Welsh Rarebit! That's what I'm having."

"Welsh rabbit?"

"It's not rabbit, its rarebit ... a kind of melted cheese sandwich. What looks good to you?"

"I think the Club sandwich and fries."

The waiter came over from another table, took their order for sandwiches and a "local beer" he recommended.

"When we finish here, I've got to meet with some of our group. So you're on your own for a few hours."

"I'll be in the pool," Jack responded.

"Good idea!"

The waiter returned with two bottles of beer and a pair of glasses.

"Tusker Lager ..." Jack said reading the label with an elephant image. Not bothering with the glass, he took a swig from the frosty bottle. His dad did the same. *"Pretty good too!"*

"It hits the spot," George responded.

"What's on our agenda, dad?"

"Well, delegates are arriving today. Tomorrow morning, the convention starts with a general assembly followed by breakout meetings … we'll see how it goes. I don't think we'll get too involved after that. The delegates have to figure out their mission, charter, bylaws and stuff. We're just helping them get started."

The waiter returned with food. George's "Welsh Rarebit" was just an open-face grilled cheese sandwich, but he relished it. And Jack had another Tusker before returning to the cottage for swim trunks.

The swimming pool was small with a diving board at the end nearest the bar which had an assemblage of patrons. Jack couldn't resist going straight to the board and making a near perfect one-and-a-half dive. Something was wrong. He too easily hit the pool bottom with his forehead. Popping to the surface, he raised his left hand above the water and saw the pinky at a right 90-degree angle. He grabbed it and snap-aligned it back into place. No one at the bar even noticed the dive. He swam around a bit and ascertained that the whole thing was only eight feet deep. It should not have had a diving board. Later that evening, his father noticed the forehead lump right at the hairline. Jack didn't think it was too noticeable as his longish hair and fuzzy red beard gave him a caveman look and bump or not, wouldn't make any difference.

In the morning, they met up with six of the IAPS group and headed to the Nairobi Parliamentary Chambers, the convention site. The place was a buzzing! Everyone was herded toward the amphitheatre and seated by delegation for the commencement address and opening of the First All Africa Advertising Professionals Society Convention. The objective for the convention was to develop the Charter for the Africa Advertising Professionals Society (AAPS).

A pressing first order of business was the decision whether to allow or deny the South Africa delegates from attending or participating. A motion to deny the South African group was tabled and a vote was immediately called. Due to South Africa's long-standing practice of Apartheid, the racial separation of black and white society, education, political powers and economic control, runs counter to what the AAPS seeks to promote. The vote was taken and the South Africans were asked to leave Kenya. After the vote, the rest of the day was "Blah ... blah ... blah ... blah." Jack and his dad bailed out of the convention as the breakout meetings started, the Charter work had to be created by their members and not influenced by the international guests.

That night, everyone was bused over to a lodge outside of Nairobi for dinner. Jack was a little surprised when the tall good looking brunette, Marilyn, slinked over to their table and sat across from Jack. She was all dolled-up with her long hair coiled up into a bun off her shoulders and war paint on. She presumably had no other place to go. A scan of the room revealed her equally gorgeous sister, Vanessa, sat pouting with her dad and no other males less than 25 years her senior were visible. Vanessa, curly blonde, was a little shorter and about two years older than her sister. Jack imagined Marilyn won the Rock-Paper-Scissors game with her sister to scout the only male prospect in the group. He was sure a full report would be made afterwards and so decided to proceed cautiously. After all, Jack felt unprepared being fresh out of college, unemployed, no assets and lack exposure to the ways of managing a sophisticated debutant girlfriend. On top of that, making light conversation was not something that he enjoyed or had much patience for, but she was persistent and undeniably attractive.

After some forgettable "blah ... blah ... blah"

topics, like her living in the small town of Chaka, California where she attended college and decided to stay after graduation. And Jack's admission that he just graduated from a college in Grainfield, Ohio, and only a few weeks back in Michigan with his folks. She confided that her sister recently took residence at the family's home in Michigan. George said nothing during most of the foregoing with the exception of acknowledging he knew her father as a Detroit Advertising practitioner.

"Oh god, I just love California! I went to college in Chaka, cute little town and I decided to stay there after graduation for awhile. I'm also back home now living with my folks. I just love Michigan don't you?" Marilyn cooed just before exposing her teeth to pull a piece of steak from her fork. It was the kind of come-on gesture intended to draw attention to her mouth as she watched Jack's eyes in reaction.

"Yeah, it's okay. Wouldn't say I 'love' it though," Jack said in a measured fashion, *"there are a lot of nice lakes, but the mosquitoes and humidity you can keep."*

"What's on for tomorrow?" she inquired.

"I don't think anything is scheduled for the whole group" Jack said, *"so we're going to make a road*

trip to Mombasa, on the coast. Another couple from our group is riding with us."

George nodded his confirmation but remained silent.

"Kind of a Banzai run down and back" Jack continued as the entrée dishes were cleared by wait staff. *"It's reported that Mt. Kilimanjaro in neighboring Tanzania will be visible in the morning about halfway there."*

"Well, that sounds exciting!" Having said that, Jack thought she may be looking for an invitation.

Desert and coffee were served and consumed with a little more chatter.

"Well, that's it for tonight," Jack announced, *"We've got an early start tomorrow morning."*

"Have a safe trip," Marilyn said, getting to her feet.

"Thank you for joining us for dinner."

As she swayed away, she glanced back over her shoulder.

"Oh, boy! That one's a handful!" George exclaimed. Jack knew he was thinking of Mr. Jameson dealing with his two daughters on this trip. Both of which

appeared to have high-maintenance personalities and financial needs to match.

The Toyota Corolla sedan was ready by the time Jack and his father made it to the lobby. Their travelling companions were a heavy set couple in their late 40s. Jack drove, on the left like they did in the U.K., George rode shotgun and the Binks occupied the back seats. Picking through the bustle of Nairobi to the highway, Jack could tell the back end of the little car squatted and the steering would be sloppy. A few miles out of town, the 4 lane divided highway turned into a two lane black asphalt ribbon with no signs or lane markings. It was a 600 mile, 8 hour round trip and he kept the pedal down. There were occasional signs indicating the kilometers to Mombasa or the next town. The Binks were chatterboxes and not found lacking of subjects to talk about. Jack kept a sharp eye on the road. No fencing existed to keep animals off the road and occasionally a water buffalo or giraffe carcass could be spotted, usually with the hulk of a burned out tanker truck nearby. They encountered many areas of such man-made debris littering the road, mostly tanker trucks. A few hours into the trip, between Makindu and Tsavo, the peak of Mt. Kilimanjaro appeared to their right.

But some clouds were beginning to form around its peak and as they were told, usually disappeared completely by noon. He pulled to the left side of the road, because they all needed a good stretch and a photo op. It was understandably very hot as Kenya is bisected by the Equator. With a little camera in hand, Jack climbed an eight foot tall mound by the side of the road. It had large holes all through it like Swiss cheese, but it was hard enough to support his weight. A short distance away, several bells could be heard like someone was herding goats. Sure enough, out of the tall shrubs, a Maasai warrior with bow, arrows and a spear jogged toward him and started shouting.

Jack hopped off the dirt mound and greeted him with "Jambo!" the Swahili salutation "hello". The Maasai would have none of this from a gringo! He kept yelling and waving his arms. George shouted for him to get back to the car. The Binks were already inside and wanted nothing to do with this situation.

Unafraid, Jack went to the car and got some colorful plastic combs that Nancy encouraged him to bring for handing out to any African kids they encounter. The simplistic thought to give something to the upset Maasai warrior was totally wrong. When he went back to the Maasai in the middle of the road and extended them. The man smacked them out of Jack's hand and continued yelling and gesturing. That made it clear that it was time to go.

Sometime later, they learned that it was perceived

as an infidel trespassing into the Maasai holy land and the warrior took it as his duty to protect it. They were told that it was lucky that the Maasai was so tolerant. Maasai warriors are not afraid of anyone and are known to take on lions with only a spear.

On reaching Mombasa, a place that was not on par with the metropolis of Nariobi, Jack parked the car and they walked amongst the stalls of an open market while looking for somewhere to get lunch. There weren't any tourism supporting businesses ... no hotels or even beach palapas for drinks or food. Aside from the main paved road to the oil depot, every other lane was rutty dirt. Off shore, oil tanker ships were anchored awaiting their turn to off load gasoline to tank trucks. This explained why so many of the rigs were burned out hulks alongside the road between Nairobi and Mombasa. The full tank trucks were driven all hours of the day and night up to Nairobi to fuel the capital. At night on the unmarked road, the drivers fatigued or blinded by darkness undoubtedly drove through herds of animals crossing or loitering in the roadway.

The return trip to Nairobi was thankfully quiet and uneventful as the Binks and George dozed most of the way. Jack lost count of the tank truck remains and animal bones which predictably clustered around every significant curve in the road.

On return to the Norfolk, Jack and George dropped into the Norfolk's bar for a few Tuskers. Already there were some of their group offering a glowing report of the sight-seeing excursion they had in Tanzania to see the Victoria Falls, a popular tourist destination. Not knowing how the experience would be described by the Binks, the two down-played the experience of the day's events. Approaching the hotel cottage, George looked at his son and muttered *"The trip they took might have been a better idea."*

The next morning, a Land Rover driving safari though conservancy lands of Tsavo National Park just outside Nairobi was the principle activity. A little band of five vehicles traversed across the savanna full of great herds of wildebeest and zebra in migration. The tall grasses gave way to rocky outcrops then dropping down to marshy ponds occupied by clusters of black rhinos, hippos and water buffalo. Again, Jack managed to get the driving duty due to left-side driving experience of the previous day. His dad took the shot gun seat. In the back bench they were to have Jan and her father, Mr. Lane. This elderly gentleman, at least a decade older than George, was the namesake son of one of the five men considered to be "the fathers of Advertising in the Modern Age." Mr. Lane seemed to be held in high regard by George and the others as a founding statesman of the APSA and soon to be President of the IAPSA. Jan, as it turned out, stayed at the Norfolk to study for her Master's degree. So, their little band of vehicles slowly crept up to various herds of buffalo, giraffes and the like while Mr. Lane stood on the back seat with his head and shoulders sticking up through the sunroof opening. His super-8 movie camera with small lens wouldn't capture enough photographic images of these animals without getting very close. Predictably, Mr. Lane kept telling Jack to get closer.

Four-wheel driving in the deep grasses near the marshy ponds occupied by the huge rhinos was a challenge. Jack kept thinking about the 1962 John Wayne movie 'Hatari', (Swahili for "Danger!"), in which a rhino gored a guy's leg and almost overturned a Land Rover like the one they occupied. These huge single horned herbivores may be up to 10 foot long, 7 foot tall at the shoulder, 10,000 pounds in weight, could run 30 miles per hour and were prone to charge with little provocation, especially in the presence of young offspring.

"We have to get closer!" he repeated without indication of which of them he was addressing. Each time, George would give his son a glance and nod to go ahead. So, Jack steered away from the convoy and drove over rough grassy terrain to get a little closer ... and closer ... and closer at Mr. Lane's prodding. They continued up to the point that their

wheels started to lose traction in the wet muck. Jack looked over at the convoy they departed and wondered who of them would come to their aid if they got stuck.

Jack drove pretty close actually seeing rhinos with some young ones, a very dangerous position to be in that they later learned. Across the pond, there were elephants, giraffe and water buffalo that made good photo backdrop for Mr. Lane's rhino shot. *"Drive over there, Jack, a little closer!"* Mr. Lane said. Jack motioned to George that it would be inevitable that they'd get stuck and not worth it. His father looked out the window at the wet ground the tires were sinking into and finally told Mr. Lane that they were as close as they can safely be. The whirring sound his little camera made had stopped and he sat back down. Jack steered the Rover very carefully to depart the marsh and return to the safety of the convoy that was stopped in the tundra at the sight of some gazelles, zebras and wildebeest. Mr. Lane was happy and that made George happy. At this point, Jack was already mentally checked-out and imagining the taste of cold Tuskers back at the Norfolk.

The next day, many of the tour group opted for a late rising with time for a leisurely breakfast and packing of baggage. The group would say goodbye to the now familiar Norfolk Hotel and move to the Treetops Lodge. Located in the western part of

Kenya inside the Aberdare National Park, Treetops was built on stilts in 1932 as it lay in the path of an ancient elephant migratory route between the Aberdare Ranges and Mount Kenya beside a natural waterhole and salt lick. This would only be a one-night stay because the only thing to do there is have dinner and drinks while watching elephants, tundra grazers and predators in the same place to lick salt blocks and drink water.

What was strange about this place is that floodlights illuminated all around the lodge area. From almost any direction, once the flood lights were on, the elephants, lion, zebra, giraffe, water buffalo and just about anything else out there came to the watering hole and to docilely drink and lick white blocks of salt surrounding the water. It was quite strange that this nocturnal activity occurred by prey and predator without the expected chase, capture and gore just in time for the entertainment of the hotel guests as they sip their cocktails and had dinner. Watching this unbelievable scenario had Jack thinking that something nefarious was afoot. He got up and walked over to a window and asked one of the hotel staff why these animals seem so docile and that he suspected the presence of drugs or something in the salt lick blocks. He said yes, the animals come for the drugs, wake up the next morning groggy, but they come back every night for more.

The group left Treetops early afternoon and had a very short ride to the next hotel, Kenyatta Safari Club. It was a chain of low profile cabins sprawled along the side of the river at the base of Mount Kenya. Almost as soon as Jack and his dad arrived at their assigned cabin, the phone chimed. It was Jan asking Jack if he wanted to join the girls in a horseback ride. She stated that tomorrow would be a hot day, so right now would be the best time to go. A few minutes later, Jack was at the stables. The horses were already saddled and ready to go. The girls and the trail guide were mounted and waiting. He was tickled by the three of them greeting him in unison, *"Hi, Jack!"*

The trail guide led them north along a trail on the east side of the river that was mostly shaded by a thick canopy of trees. Jan rode just in front of Jack in the single column behind the guide. She was the first to notice the sweet smell of the marijuana cigarette the guide lit up.

"Say! That smells really good!" she called to the guide.

"Absolutely!" Jack seconded enthusiastically.

"Yeah! Care to share that?" came from Vanessa riding behind Jack.

The slow procession of the column continued as

the spliff was puffed and passed around affording everyone a mild buzz which they profusely thanked the guide for providing.

The horses seemed content to plod along.

Jan paced her horse next to Jack at one point. *"I want to thank you for driving my dad around yesterday,"* she said, *"He told me he had a great time!"*

"Yeah, sure was exciting!" he lied.

"He can be a real pain sometimes, so, thanks for putting up with him."

"But what happened to you?" Jack asked. *"We thought you'd be coming with him."*

"I'm in my second year of working for my Masters degree and can't wait to get it over with," Jan said.

"What school?" Vanessa joined in. On closer examination, she appeared to be a year or two older than Jack and her sister, but she had the right look and attributes, he thought.

"Princeton"

"How close are you to the finish?" Jack asked.

"This summer! The last two courses ... both hard ones. I had to do it because they're required, everybody has to take them, and seats are limited, "Jan said.

"That's why ... the books?" Vanessa inquired.

"I have to!"

"Marilyn and I are going to the pool for a little sun later. You can join us and read there."

"Okay!" Jan responded.

"How about you, Jack?" Vanessa asked.

"Uhhh .... Yeah, maybe ..." he answered.

The trail continued along the river for several miles and came to an open field that had been cleared of brush forming a small aircraft landing strip. About 100 yards into the clearing, the guide waved his arm to stop. At the opposite end of the airstrip the odd trumpeting and snorting sounds increased just before the elephants appeared. The herd crossed at the other end of the airstrip. It was another small elephant herd of about 10 adults and two young ones depart the riverbank on their left in the direction of open meadows and scattered trees to the right.

"Don't move, be quiet and they will go," said the guide.

"They may not see us. But! ...... can't always be sure with little ones."

Just then a large long-tusk pachyderm turned toward the riders and stopped. Its ears were straight out as if to charge. Knowing an average East African elephant's height of 13 feet, Jack tried to guess the distance that separated the horseback riders from the 11 ton beast.

The guide spoke in a low voice, *"Okay ... we go now."* He turned his horse around signaling for the others to follow.

The elephant studied them but didn't move. A few minutes later they were back under the tree canopy. It was a welcomed relief as the temperature was on the rise and the sun was already burning. The riders saw many animals slake their thirst on the return trail segment. At the stables, they parted ways to their respective cabins with tentative confirmations of the pool side gathering later.

Once inside the air conditioned cabin, Jack flopped on the bed and slept. Startled by the ringing phone, he picked it up. It was Vanessa, *"Jack, we went to the pool, but it was uncomfortably Hot!"*

"Oh! Geeze! What time is it? I fell asleep!"

"You didn't miss anything. We were there for like 3 minutes and left" she said, *"And way too easy to get burned. The hotel desk said morning is the best pool time. So ... tomorrow morning then?"*

"Sounds like a plan," he answered and returned the handset to its base.

In the evening, just like at Treetops, this hotel offers a dining experience with a river view. Picture windows face the river with a large tree on the other side. One of the trees limbs extends far over the water and is often occupied by a leopard sitting on the most horizontal segment of the limb and illuminated by spotlights. That is where a goat or gazelle carcass is placed every day. As if on cue, the leopard appeared on the limb and devoured the fresh killing. There were some small visitors looking for a drink and paid no attention to the big cat. Jack found it a bit funny ... the people were eating ... the cat was eating ... looking at each other through panes of glass ... maybe the leopard would like a dash of A1 Sauce?

Today they were to leave this hotel, but unlike the Treetops early departure, they wouldn't depart until mid-afternoon, at which time the tour group will go to the Nairobi airport for a dinner flight to Johannesburg, South Africa. Jack was restless and had to do something, so he decided to go for a little jog. After raising a little sweat, maybe that's when he'd make an appearance at the pool. It was already too hot to wear a t-shirt, so he went in running shorts, sneakers and a head band. The three girls were there all on their stomachs sans bikini top straps and doused in sun oil. Jan, as expected, had a textbook open.

"Good morning!" he greeted.

"Morning"

"Hi, Jack"

"Yeah! Comfortable right now!" he declared.

"Feel the pool temperature," Marilyn said.

He bent down and stuck his hand in. *"Warm, but a little cooler than the air right now,"* he reported, *"... and surely will feel cooler yet when I get back."*

"Where are you going?" Marilyn asked.

"I'm feeling a little restless, so I'm just going out for a jog ... probably back in 20 minutes."

"Okay"

"Have fun"

Jack left the pool area and followed a dirt footpath. He was headed toward a grassy meadow with large trees, the branches of which go to the ground and look like giant bushes. A few yards beyond the cabins and small buildings there was a deep ditch. *"Must be a drainage or plumbing project,"* he thought. There was a narrow plank that lay across the trench which he used to cross over the 6 or 7 foot wide chasm, that was equally as deep.

He did some standing stretches to loosen up and hopped about like a prizefighter to prestart the run up of his heart rate. Starting at a small step easy jog pace, he headed down a flattened grass pathway with tire tracks. As the grass became progressively taller, his thoughts of a snake encounter loomed. Continuing on but focused on the ground, he rounded another 'bush-tree' to see a baby elephant 20 plus yards away. He instantly stopped and turned around to catch a glimpse of its mommy or daddy tusker just a little further away. *"Holy Shit!"* Its ears were straight out to the sides of its head and were motionless for a second the elephant spotted him, and then it charged!

"Oh! FFFFUUUUCCCKKKKK!!!" Jack ran as fast as he could and it was gaining on him. It let out a trumpeting blast and loud snorts as it gave chase. Around another 'bush-tree' ... trumpet blasts, snorting, and now the thumping of those wide, flat feet. An involuntary glance over the shoulder was

filled with a trunk waving around between those long tusks stretching to get a hold of him! He had to do a 100 plus yard dash in front of a locomotive closing fast! He could make out the roof line of the lodge ahead as he stumbled, but caught himself from falling down.

"Oh, God!" he thought, *"Just get me outta this and I'll be good, really, really good!"*

Just ahead was the drainage ditch with the plank across it. He could feel the animal's hot breath on his back as he jumped.

Jack hit the opposite side of the ditch at solar plexus level, knocking the wind out of him. Despite not being able to breathe, he pulled up just enough to roll on his side above the ditch. The elephant was pissed and its trunk and long tusks were just inches away. The smelly moist breath from the animals' trunk blasted him as it waved about just out of reach. It stomped the ground ... made a few trumpet toots ... shook its head and then left. He lay on the ground until he could breathe again.

"That's what the ditch is for!! It's a dry moat to keep the animals from wandering onto the hotel grounds!"

"Holy Shit!" he thought, *"... of course! There aren't*

any pipes lying around. Jesus, how STUPID OF ME! Damn, I can't tell anyone about this."

Composure regained, he stood up and noticed dirt covering a large scrape from his pecs to waist. He certainly wasn't going to the pool now and the still tender lump on his forehead from the last pool confirmed it. *The last thing he needed was to have them think he was the idiot that he felt like right now! And definitely didn't want this event to be told to the rest of the group and embarrass his Dad.*

Jack made it back to the cabin without being spotted and hopped into the shower. The scrapes weren't bloody, only rubbed red. *"Maybe not so visible after a few days,"* he hoped. With a couple of hours before the groups planned departure, his bags packed, the hotel bar's cold Tuskers were calling. Every gulp of suds became a rewind & replay of his 'jog.' It was the third bottle that he focused on its label and decided to keep it as a souvenir to his third life. Carefully wrapped in some clothing in his travel bag, he was confident it would make it back stateside.

After making the journey to the Johannesburg Intercontinental Hotel, father and son went up to the panoramic penthouse bar for night caps ... every night they were there. The days in Johannesburg were filled with tours, the De Beers Diamond Mine, a gold mine, a cattle ranch and a road trip to Cape Town. Their last night before the long flight to Amsterdam, they decided to have a 'Farewell Funguel' in the hotel bar. It was a busy place and felt lucky to grab the last two empty stools at the bar. About 10 minutes later, George had to go the restroom. That was when an older gent in his 50s next to Jack spoke.

"You're an American!"

"Yes, sir," Jack answered, curious as to why he asked.

"You! Americans come down here aren't wanted." It was evident the man had a lot to drink. *"You think you can tell us how to run things, but you're wrong! You don't know! An ya know what pisses us off? Yer all a bunch of hypocrites!"*

At that moment, Jack and George were unaware that a photo of them voting in Nairobi to expel the South Africans made front page news.

"Uh, what? I don't know what you are talking about, sir."

"Yes you do! Interfering with our govament, laws, society ..." A younger man about Jacks age on the other side of this fellow said, "Come-on dad. It's time to go."

"I'm not finished yet," he said, *"You Americans are ignorant to whatch been going on here for decades! We built and developed ... there'd be nothing here without us South Afrikaners. We raised the standard of living for everybody ... unlike your country."*

"What?"

"Look, dad, he doesn't know ... let's just go!" the younger man said.

"I bet you don't even know your own history! How do you think ...?"

The younger man stood up and pulled the intoxicated man away. He looked at Jack and said *"Sorry!"*

George came back just as the two of them left.

"Something happen?" he asked.

"I guess the guy and his son overheard our accent as American and felt compelled to make a statement defending Apartheid."

The bartender saw what transpired and approached. George ordered another round.

"That guy had a bit much, sorry," the bartender said.

"It's okay now," Jack responded, *"His son wasn't going to let it go too far."*

Placing the new drinks on the bar, the bartender said, *"Say, would you fellows like to see a play? It's for free! Another guy just left these two tickets with me that he couldn't use tonight."*

"Sure!" George said, *"What's the play?"*

The bartender stepped over to the register and returned with the tickets. *"If you're going to make it, you'd have to go now,"* he said. *"Grab a cab from the lobby; it's a few miles from here."*

They gulped their drinks, thanked the bartender and saw an entertaining but forgettable performance.

They arrived in Amsterdam late. Jack said goodbye to Jan as she got ready to take the next flight back to Princeton. Everyone else, it appeared, would be departing in the morning including her dad, Mr. Lane.

After breakfast, George grabbed his bag and left for the airport to catch a late morning flight to JFK. Jack was staying in Europe to sight-see for another week. He left the hotel and strolled about the canals of Amsterdam. The free Heineken brewery tour ended with a complimentary beer sampling which he couldn't pass up. It was about 3 pm in the hotel room that he got an unexpected phone call.

"Jack! Oh god, I'm glad you're still here."

"Vanessa, what's up?"

"We're in trouble because we stayed in the room too long. We're trying to leave for the airport but the porter said we have to pay for another night! But, we can get out of it if we can say we're just moving into your room. Is that okay?"

"Uh, yeah, okay."

"Great! We'll be right over!"

Less than five minutes after hanging up, there was a knock at the door. Marilyn and Vanessa, dressed to the nines in long floral pattern cotton dresses, heels and wide brimmed floppy hats entered in a flurry and threw their arms around Jack while a suspicious looking porter with their baggage waited. Jack and the two girls stepped back into the room for the porter to bring in the cart of bags and unload.

"Marilyn took too long in the bathroom!"

"Vanessa, you got up too late to shower!"

"These ladies are staying with you?"

"Yes … they are," Jack lied.

With a very skeptical look, the porter left the room with his cart and closed the door behind him.

"Thank you, Jack"

"So where are the two of you headed?"

"Ireland and Scotland!"

Jack revealed, "Tomorrow morning I'll hop a train to Germany … visit with my grandfather for a few days and then a few more days with an exchange student my Mom hosted and her family."

Vanessa peeked out of the room door. The porter had left. *"Okay Marilyn, time to go,"* she announced.

In another flurry, hugs and kisses and they were gone. He got a rise out of the whole episode but it was too fast. Only the lingering scent of Marilyn's perfume remained.

Jack's grandfather, Rolph, met him at the train station. During the next few days he would rent a car and Jack drove them to nearby castles to walk around. His last night with Grandpa, his live-in companion Golda, (somehow related to Rolph, but Jack never figured it out), prepared a nice dinner and there were some guests. Everything transpired in German so he was a bit disconnected. One of the guests was an attractive twenty-two year old dental hygienist, who happened to be his cousin! She had an athletic build, short dark red hair and an acceptable command of English. After dinner, they went to a dance club and encountered some of her friends. She was cute and seemed to like him by the kind of kiss he received before leaving him at the door to his Grandpa's apartment. Passing ships in the dark? It was too late in their brief encounter to make anything of it. Kissing cousins? Oh, well ... back to the train station.

Nadja, (their exchange student) met him at the train station about mid-day. Tall, slender-figured with dark eyes and long straight black hair. Her nose was a little beakish and against the background of high cheek bones, she appeared a bit gaunt. Jack had only seen her briefly at the Auburn house, but it was enough that he could recognize her and act in a friendly and familiar manner.

Nadja was multi-linguistic and could converse in English, French, Spanish, Italian, and of course, German. She was an only child and a bit of a prattle box, he got the impression that he was somehow considered a prospect ... or someone to practice upon. Everything about him, everything about her, everything about everything was constantly machine gunned into conversation. He liked her sweetness and thoughtfulness. So it was tough for him to endure the intensity of the barrage and retain much of what was said. He could tell when her father, Frank, was mentally checking out. It seemed to him he practiced this self-preservation escape often, Nadja's mom, Olivia, was a chatterbox herself.

The days passed quickly, and Jack again stood on a train platform, this time to return to Amsterdam. He had a little time to kill before the train arrived. He glanced about the little shops proximate to the station when a familiar image caught his attention. It was a wall mounted sign in the shape of a red square with diagonal white stripe denoting the international maritime "Divers Down" flag. It has common usage in identifying recreational SCUBA Diving businesses. Jack's newly achieved certification and diving interest drew him toward it. A small display window next to the sign had several breathing regulators and sales prices visible. The remaining three Traveler's Checks in his pocket would be enough to start equipping his new hobby.

The shop keeper was anxious to make a sale and agreed to sell him the featured Spanish-made Nimrod regulator for the three twenty dollar checks he had. On the train to the Amsterdam airport, he happily tossed his new acquisition into his travel bag only to cringe seconds later when he heard glass break.

Sure enough, the Tusker bottle wrapped in a t-shirt was the casualty.

THE BLENDER

J ack had carefully arranged his final semester at Denton to be with no academic load and only Pottery 101, Beginning Saxophone and a Physical Education requirement he had to complete for graduation. So he took Scuba Diving Certification with significant pool time! While most of his classmates were busting butt taking the heavy-duty lab sciences for graduation, he was in a pressure free bubble. His last days amounted to throwing a little mud onto a spinning wheel, blurting a few notes on the horn and hanging out at the pool.

After commencement, he was ready to get the Open Water Certification that had several achievement segments focusing on Shore Entry, Wreck Diving, Cave Diving, Swift Water and more. Back in Michigan for the summer, the local dive shop organized classes and opportunities to meet other like minded peeps through which he teamed with Jimmy Andrews as a dive buddy.

Jimmy lived about a mile from their house and

a mutual interest in SCUBA diving led to a lot of time together before and after classes. He was about Jack's height and size, blond hair, blue eyes, a square jaw line and a couple of years younger. They became the best of friends. Jack spent a bit of time at Jimmy's house as he had a twin sister Jack thought attractive. He was occasionally rewarded with her cameo appearances with her usual best friend, Samantha. Jack confessed his interest in Jimmy's sister on more than one occasion and was routinely rebuffed.

"You don't know what you're talking about! She's a pain in the ass! She already has a boyfriend! You don't want to have anything to do with her! She'll drive you nutz!" he repeatedly admonished Jack's amorous mentions.

Sophia's best friend and shadow, Samantha, lived two houses over and he'd only refer to her as a "neighbor kid". The two girls were more like twins than Jimmy and Sophia. Both of them were a little Tom-boyish, liked motorcycling, and had a similar quirky sense of humor, athletic and blond. Sophia had shoulder length hair and was a bit hefty 18 year old girl with blossoming parts. In contrast, Samantha wore her hair to her butt, slimmer and looked to be about 13 years old. During the summer, Jack would see them both at parties and bars and was initially shocked that Samantha was of 'legal age'. He later learned that Samantha did things that Sophia didn't, like SCUBA diving, motorcycling and snow skiing.

Eventually, Jimmy told Sophia of Jack's interest in her. It was much later that Jack learned Sophia had no such interest in him ... but Samantha did! It explained why time and again when Jack maneuvered toward Sophia; he would invariably find himself with Samantha. He was the fool of their deceptive plans! It took him awhile, but he learned that Samantha was much more interesting than her best friend ... more on that later.

But today, Jimmy and Jack were on a mission, to get Open Water Certified as fast as they could. And an important component was the Swift Water Certification event in which each of them had to demonstrate learned skills to entering, exiting, maneuvering and navigation. The first dive would be a super-easy low current familiarization.

They had just gone under for the second scuba dive of the day. It almost didn't matter what time of the year they dove in the Great Lakes, the water was always cold. But this was early-October, and this water was well mixed as it flowed through the Saint Clair River under the Blue Water Bridge in Port Huron, Michigan. The warmer surface temperatures were churned up with the frigid water below the thermo cline gave them a balmy 55-degree water temperature that was consistent from top to bottom.

A six-foot tether line was tied to Jack's left wrist, at the other end, his dive partner's right wrist. Although Jack wanted to dive with his best friend, Jimmy, the Dive Shop dive master, Tony, split them up and Jack got paired with Bobby Hudson, aka - "Goofy". Jack told himself that Tony wanted to separate his two best divers and therefore keep some level of control over the cadre of squids comprising today's Open Water Diver class. Admittedly, Jimmy and Jack had gotten more than a little over-confident and aggressive in some of the other Open Water Certification events. They often talked about becoming Dive masters themselves, even though they had both only achieved the Basic Certification five months ago.

The plan was to enter the water just under the Blue Water Bridge and using some techniques to slow the effect of the current and travel perhaps a few thousand yards downstream to an exit point. After the first run, Goofy ... err, Bob and Jack had only accumulated fisherman's lead sinkers and a railroad spike from the rocky channel bottom. They both wanted something more ... bragger's rights. Bob by the way, got his nickname because he resembled the Disney character ... tall, lanky, walked like a duck and had a severe overbite. Apparently not knowing how or why the nickname stuck, he accepted it and was happy to be recognized, accepted and included as good-guy by the diving crew. Jack never called him "Goofy" to his face.

As on the first dive, Bob and Jack faced into the current and slowly bottom crawled to the right that led deeper toward the center of the channel. The more they moved toward the center of the channel, the faster the current and darker it got. The water moved fast, it was hard to even look for artifacts on the bottom. Even though it was just past noon and the overhead sunlight produced the greatest luminescence, within the circle of their visibility, everything was a dark olive green. Looking to the right, they could only make out darkness of the increased depth beyond a few yards.

"Underwater visibility is just ten-to-fifteen feet," said Tony, the Dive master during the pre-dive briefing. *"Along the sides of the river, the current speed was just one-and-a-half to two miles per hour. That means you will be moving at three feet per second … giving you about three or four seconds to see and react at that range of visibility."*

"Also, be aware of possible submerged dock pilings and other metal objects in the water," he emphasized.

Jack felt Bob tug on the line. He turned his gaze left to see Bob signal to go further right. Already putting some of the swift-water basics learned from their previous dive, they went deeper. The current kept the river bottom rocky and clear of sediment. It was easy going.

Two weeks ago, the dive shops other Dive Master, Marvin, had concluded the class covering Underwater Navigation, Wreck Diving, Night Diving and Rescue/Recovery Diving. It was then Marvin announced the "clincher" for this event and they all wanted to attend. The divers all signed-up on the spot, interested in finding the Prohibition-Era bottles of Whiskey that were rumored to still be at the bottom of the river, corks intact and full.

These prizes are rumored to be in open view on the bottom as the swift current kept sediment from accumulating. So, these trophies should be easy to find, they thought.

In winter months, the river froze over, and booze runners from Canada often broke through the ice and sank their heavily laden cars as they tried to drive across it. Other times when it flowed and the hooch went by long boat, law enforcement often rammed the bootleggers' boats when they tried to make a run for it ... or, more often than not, as the feds closed in, the evidence was ditched over the side. All of which had happened under the cover of darkness or blindness of a heavy snow fall to cross from Canada to the U.S.

During the pre-dive talk, an ore-ship was chugging its way North in the channel.

"Okay," Tony said clearing his throat. *"As you can*

see, there'll be traffic," pointing to the ship, "most of them are about five hundred to seven hundred feet long. Some of the biggest are a thousand feet long, a hundred feet wide with twin props producing 20,000 horsepower! In the channel, they mostly steer using bow thrusters. Those are perpendicular pipes from one side of the bow to the other with a thousand horsepower engine to spin a propeller in the middle of the pipe to create a side pressure! On the inside of a turn, water is sucked in like a vacuum and discharged in torrent on the other side to move the bow. So ... stay away from the bow as you could be sucked in or blasted away depending on which side you find yourself. Keep in mind that fully loaded, they have a twenty to thirty foot draft. That means ... there may only be a twenty foot clearance between the keel and river bottom."

Forty feet down, the water temperature did get colder. Jack guessed that they were nearing the center of the channel. His eyes were adjusting to the dim light as they continued deeper. They finally reached a flat spot on the bottom. The current was really strong and Jack latched onto the top of a triangular boulder. There was a sweet-spot next to the boulder that got him out of the current stream and he could hang there without too much effort. Bob also dug his hands and fins into the bottom to hang on at their position.

"Haaa …. Haaa …. Haaa"

Jack turned to look at Bob. He was making the noise. Jack could see Bob's free hand clutch his air pressure gauge. "Haaa … Haaa … Haaakk" He let go of the gauge and fiddled with the secondary stage of his air regulator.

A faint rumbling noise began to get much louder and louder. "Haawwkk … Haawwkkk … Hawwkkk" the noise was not made by Bob, it was his "sonic" regulator warning of low tank pressure!

"Damn! He has an eighty cubic foot aluminum tank to my steel seventy-two," Jack thought, *"and he's out of air?"*

Bob gestured to surface. Jack shook his head "NO!"

In a matter of seconds, the rumbling noise was so loud; it was like they were standing in a steel stamping factory. It was getting darker by the second!

"Haawwnnkk … Haawwnnkk" Jack turned to look up at the surface. The dark green dot of the sun was being eclipsed by the bow of a ship! The ship's bow point grew wider and wider until they were in almost total darkness. A fleeting thought of a bow thruster sucking in and blowing out a huge volume of water kept him glued to the channel bottom. He tugged on the tether line for Bob to move closer gesturing that he would flip Bob's reserve air valve behind his head on the tank.

He moved closer and under Jack, clinging to the rocks. Jack reached down and turned the J-valve beneath the primary regulator. His secondary went silent ... he thought ... he couldn't tell ... the rumbling overhead was making the riverbed vibrate ... Jack could feel it though the boulder his right hand gripped. Turbines ... Diesels ... Stamping Steel ... Furnaces ... Rattling Chains ... Crunching Rocks ... Earth Movers!!!

Jack clung to the boulder with both hands now. Bob lost grip on the bottom and was dangling at the end of the tether line! The increased drag on the boulder was trenching the rocky riverbed. Jack kept his head down and fin-kicked as hard as he could, but the trenching of the riverbed continued.

It quickly got light and he noticed how fast the trenching sediment streamed off in the current. Suddenly ... they were in a whirlpool! Jack smashed into Bob and they swirled like socks in a washing machine ... elbow ... knees ... head ... tank ... Jack's mask got pushed down around his neck. He chomped on the mouthpiece so hard his upper and lower teeth were touching. Swirl ... swirl ... swirl.

He let go of Bob and got the mask on again. As

he blew water out of it, he could still make out the river bottom moving swiftly past. He was in good shape and they grabbed the bottom again facing into the current. Instinctively they made a fast crawl along the bottom to the left back to the shoulder of the river. Bob finds a white object and places into the small canvas bag hanging from his waist.

Moving to the left … now back to thirty-five foot depth. Jack tugs on the tether and gives him the "Okay" hand signal. He does the same.

"Haaaa … Haaaa … Haaaa" Bob signals to surface. Jack shakes his head "NO!" and motion to keep crawling.

Depth gauge reads twenty-two feet … they bottom crawl like scalded cats now! "Haaakkk … Haaakkk"

Up to a depth of about fifteen feet, Jack signaled to surface. Bob is out of air. Jack handed him his regulator to breathe. Bob gulped some air and handed it back. They did this a few times more as they made for the surface. Since Jack still had air, he inflated his buoyancy compensator at the surface to float. He held on to Bob so that he could manually blow air into his vest. They surfaced right next to a Coast Guard Cutter.

The next thing they knew, they were getting

hollered at by a pier full of sailors. There was a ramp nearby they swam toward and climbed.

"We don't need to tell Tony about this," Jack said, *"We need to get this part of the certification signed off."*

"Got it," he replied.

As if on cue, Tony shows up in the white cargo van and hustles the two divers out of the area before the sailors alert the officers of their presence.

As they toss their gear into the van, there was a great sigh of relief, *"We made it!"* Bob's tank was flat out of air.

"You two are about a half mile past the pickup point," Tony scolded them.

Jack looked at Bob, *"What did you find?"*

He opened the canvas bag and handed to Jack a perfect white desert plate. It had a thin blue line that ran along the rim to a small blue ship insignia on it with a French name. He imagined that a passenger or crew of a Canadian ore ship took a dinner desert from the galley out on deck or up to the bridge and accidently dropped it over the side. Despite the swift current, it sat patiently on the river bottom until Bob happened upon it.

As was their tradition after diving, Jimmy and Jack powered down a few beers.

"Another one completed!" Jimmy saluted and clinked their bottles together.

"Tony signed my Swift Water Certification, I don't think he would have done that if he found out what Bob and I did."

"Huh? What did you do?" Jimmy asked, *"Tell me, this has to be good!"*

Jack told him about wandering out to mid-channel … Bob running out of air … the ship passing over the top of them … the violent turbulence of the ship's propellers that smashed and tangled them together and tearing off Jack's mask … surfacing under the Coast Guard Cutter … and buddy-breathing.

"You guys dam near bought it!"

"We were lucky," Jack admitted, *"and now I need another beer!"*

In a rare moment of weakness, Jimmy bought another round of suds. Jack asked him to keep the incident confidential and he agreed.

"So, what's Sophia up to these days?" Jack asked, changing the subject.

"She's still at U of M in Ann Arbor, I hardly see her now. Samantha is going to Wayne State in Detroit. And I'm taking some stuff at Oakland Community," Jimmy moaned. "She'll be home for Thanksgiving."

Jimmy looked like a beaten puppy and said, "I really don't want to do this school thing."

"Take it one day at a time," Jack suggested, "before you know it, you'll have a degree."

"So, what are you up to? … more school?"

"I've been looking for work, but nothing seems to be working out at this point," Jack said, thinking about the lack of wisdom and marketability of an undergraduate English degree.

"So what's next? Can you use your dad's influence to get a job in advertising or at the "Tri-Motor Car Company?"

"I haven't got experience or education they require. But, I've been thinking about going into the NAVY," Jack confessed. "I'd like to get into their diving program. And because of my college degree, I'd go in as an officer and maybe get to see more of the world."

"Have you checked it out? It sounds like a great idea!"

"No, not yet, I ought to talk with the recruiting guys and get the low-down."

Jack's job search had not produced any good leads or interviews. George, trying to be encouraging, said that businesses look at a military service favorably and that it could be a good resume builder. Like Jimmy said, the crew went off to school and his social life stopped cold. A few weeks later, Jack called the NAVY recruiting office in Detroit and made an appointment.

Jimmy and Jack continued diving together through November when he wasn't working or attending classes. They even made a few dollars by recovering shotguns and gear that some duck hunters lost in the St. Claire River near Harsen's Island in Algonac. In the dark early morning hours, three hefty men and bags of shotguns and gear overloaded a little 8' duck boat. It was so overloaded they took on water from the surface chop and it was soon overturned. It was an easy job. Approached in the parking lot as they pulled out the tanks, the men were anxious to recover expensive shotguns and equipment. They were taken to the spot in a powerboat they arranged and within 10 minutes Jack and Jimmy were handing up the items from the water's surface into grateful hands. Most convenient, the marina bar was open when they got back!

A week before Thanksgiving, the phone rang, it was Sophia!

"Hi, Jack! How's it going?" she cooed.

"Hi Sophia ... going okay ... looks like I'll be joining the NAVY after New Years."

"I see we've got to get updated on you. Do you like plays?"

"You know you're talking to an English major ... yes, I like plays!"

"Good! I've got two tickets to "The Chocolate Soldier" for this Friday. Want to go?"

"Sure!" Jack replied enthusiastically, thinking that she'd finally come to her senses.

"Great! Pickup Samantha at 7 o'clock, she'll have the tickets!" Sophia pronounced and promptly hung up.

"Whaaat?" Jack said aloud to no one. "Wait a sec." He dialed her house back .... Busy signal. Dialed again .... Busy, and again .... Busy ... Busy. There was no getting through. He resigned himself to being a gentleman and seeing the date bamboozle through its due course.

Jack was pleasantly surprised Friday when he picked Samantha up. She was all dolled-up. Gone was the 13 year old tomboy. A dress, heels and a little makeup transformed "the neighbor kid" into an attractive young woman.

"Wow Samantha, you look great!"

She blushed and responded, "Yeah, you look sporty, too!"

They exited her house and headed to his car parked in the driveway. "What time do your folks want you home tonight?" he asked.

"My dad set no curfew for me, whenever I get home."

"And your mom is okay with that?"

"My mom doesn't live here. She's been gone for three years. My sister left right after my mom did. So, it's just my brother, my dad and I." She shrugged.

"Well, I don't want to cause a problem. It's always good to know the rules."

"My dad trusts me and my judgment. I'm putting myself through college. I have a job as a chef in a restaurant and that pays for my car, motorcycles, insurance, books, tuition and other expenses."

"Wow, I'm impressed. And, you ride, too?"

"I have a motorcycle license and two bikes … one street and one dual-sport."

"Jimmy tells me you're SCUBA certified, too"

"Yeah, last year my brother and I with some friends got certified together."

Jack began to realize that there was much more to her than Jimmy let on. She was funny, polite, thoughtful, inquisitive, independent, stubborn and unafraid of trying new things. When Jack told her where he lived, she admitted to walking along the railroad tracks near their backyard corral, with Sophia, Jimmy and her brother, Greg. They stopped and spotted the pony, chickens and sheep. Greg suggested they sneak down the backyard and the possibility of conducting a raid to steal some eggs, but didn't get around to it. "Garaging" was more fun. Kids walked the neighborhood and looked for open garages with no one around. One or more of them would be lookout while others entered the garage and find some stored beer or wine. Then, a short distance away at their clubhouse in the woods and the running stream of the Rouge River would cool the beverage.

The play at Oakland University was well performed. Afterwards, they had a couple of drinks at the Back

Seat Bar. Before he knew it, they were smooching their 'good nights' on the front step of her home.

He imagined her dad peeking through the window coverings at them, so he wanted to be observed as "respectful."

"Is your dad watching us?"

"No," she whispered, "he probably went to bed already."

"Well, thank you for the invitation. I had a really nice time tonight. And ... thank Sophia for setting it up, too."

As they kissed again, his right hand slid down to her butt. It felt tight.

"Oh, no!" he whispered, "I better leave before I get into trouble!"

"So ... get yourself into trouble," she coo'd.

But as fate would have it, Jack was about to depart home for Officer Candidate School in Newport, Rhode Island to commence a 4-year NAVY hitch. Samantha was a freshman in a 4-year undergraduate program at Wayne State. The courtship would have to wait.

THE GRAY GUNSHIP

For a moment, he stopped pushing air across the reed. Everything was dead silent ... not an echo or anything audible ... certainly no one else was out there in a boat. He strained to hear any reaction to his playing ... especially the way sound travels over water ... nothing, except a faint white noise, like what you hear in a forest when heavy snow is falling.

The ominous presence of the Buoy in the thick colorless fog seemed like it was watching him. He sat back down in the little boat and noticed that it had drifted ever so slightly closer towards the buoy.

The smooth glass-like surface of the water began to show little bumps of something just below. It took a moment for his eyes to adjust and distinguish the ghostly apparitions as translucent jellyfish rose from the depths. They had long slender tentacles and a thin pink ribbon outlining the four-leaf clover design of their umbrella shaped heads. It was still a little early in the season for these jellies to show up in the Great Peconic Bay in number, he thought.

It's usually August when unaware swimmers and downed water skiers get the painful surprise and stinging skin irritations of their stealthy presence.

The silver sax was covered in fog mist. Jack didn't care about the moisture. The horn is always slobberingly wet on the inside and has to be swabbed and the leather key pads dried after any playing. But this time it was dripping on the outside like it was just coated with a satin finish. Good thing the moisture wasn't salty. The wall hanger was still a playable instrument, but it had collected dust and the misting was just the thing to make him clean the neglected horn before hanging it up on the wall again. He shifted the horn in his lap as he reached for the thermos. A long swig of the still hot coffee reminded him of his NAVY service, standing long hours at watch on the ship's bridge with only coffee and cigarettes to keep alert.

Going into the NAVY was a pivotal decision that changed his trajectory through life. Jack wanted to continue diving as a possible career, travel and "build his resume" with achievements. Well, that wasn't to be … the NAVY "lost" his medical records and he was closed out of the diving eligibility. So instead of getting command of a Fleet Tugboat or assigned to a Salvage Ship, he was assigned to a Guided Missile Destroyer, home ported in San Diego, as the Gunnery Officer. Needless to say, Jack didn't like the big change in career paths, but Southern California sounded like an attractive destination. He wasn't sure that Gunnery amounted to translatable skills for post-military employment. But then again, diving skills might not be that marketable either.

After almost a year in NAVY schools for Surface Warfare Training and Gunnery, he had a couple of weeks to burn before reporting to the ship. So a cross country drive to San Diego was in order. The Bachelor Officer Quarters of the 32nd Street Ship Base, National City, allowed him to drive around San Diego and take some beginning flying lessons for a private pilot's license.

When he finally caught up with his ship in Olongapo, Philippines, he was not prepared for the hazing every junior officer had to endure. They had him running on "special assignments" all over the ship for days.

Jack had to investigate and report to the Weapons Department Officer, his immediate superior, three conditional statuses of the ship that were overdue to high command. The reason for the tardy reporting was attributed to his alleged late reporting for duty on the ship. The first of these required that he find the Chief Boatswain's mate and conduct an inventory of left hand spanner wrenches. Alerted beforehand, when Jack finally found him, the Chief Petty Officer berated the inquest as a huge time waste and that our idiot Captain didn't know what he's asking for ... as there was no such thing as left or right handed spanners on a Destroyer. He said the last ship the Captain was assigned to was a WWII Tug/Fire Boat that did have such arcane devices. Modern day ships had universal wrenches that could be used in either direction for connecting fire hoses to the saltwater fire main. Jack's problem, he said, was in educating the Captain about this ship and the worthlessness of the weekly report.

Jack's second assignment was to take inventory of the light locker, also a critical item of the weekly status report. He had not been aboard a ship before and wasn't exposed to the common knowledge such as spanner wrenches and light lockers. A light locker is a short section of hallway painted flat black with black curtains to keep interior light from escaping when an exterior hatch is opened. It's a visible detection countermeasure for night time. There were a dozen or more and none of them had any contents.

And lastly, he had to prepare a "Bilge Report" and deliver it to the Captain. It was overdue and he was told most important for the Captain to get it right away. It's so important that he should interrupt the Captain immediately even if it meant entering the Captain's stateroom in without knocking and deliver the verbal report because the results were needed

by the Squadron Commander. The consequences of
failure would most likely see the Captain removed
from command and the ship decommissioned as
unseaworthy. He had to visually inspect every inch
of the ships keel length inside the hull, measure the
amount of water, record the compartment number
and hull condition. This inspection took hours,
was physically impossible due to gun magazines,
Fuel tanks and other compartments under other
divisions control. Access to these compartments
was usually denied by the Officer in charge of the
space. Reporting to his senior officer who assigned
this function resulted in an alert to the Captain, Jack
was on the way to report the results. As told, he
entered the Captain's Quarters without knocking.
It interrupted a staged meeting between the
Captain and the Executive Officer discussing Courts
Marshalling Jack's boss and planning a raid on the
Chief Petty Officers' Mess to find the hidden stash
of booze. Naturally, Jack was dressed-down for
entering the Captains Quarters without knocking,
his uniform completely soiled, the shoddy results
and presentation of his findings, and how he's
responsible if the ship gets decommissioned!

After dinner in the Wardroom, the Executive Officer
ordered a Junior Officer to recite the function of
the Divisions Officers Notebook. While the Ensign
stood and spoke, everyone in the Wardroom
engaged in loud conversations about criminal

activity aboard ship. He was ordered to "shut up and sit down." Jack dreaded being next. Too late! He was ordered to provide background information about himself and why he arrived late in reporting to the ship for duty. As Jack spoke, the same thing happened. Everyone engaged in conversations about how some officer's incompetence resulted in injuries to the crew. The expression on Jack's face alerted them that he was completely stressed and had enough. Jack was ordered to sit while everyone else stood up. The Executive Officer led the Wardroom in the hymn of the evening.

They all stared at Jack and in a monk-like manner chanted in unison and pointed at him, *"Him! ... Him! Fuck Him!"*

He felt like barging for the door and escaping! The Captain smiled and put his hand out to shake.

"You Passed the test! Welcome to the Wardroom!" he laughed.

"Look at his expression!" the Executive Officer pointed at Jack's face.

"None of it was real", the Weapons Officer said, *"You can relax now."*

Another voice in the room said, *"You get to do it to the next new officer!"*

... and so ended the hazing of Ensign Springer.

Then the ship went out into the South China Sea and braved a raging Stage 5 Typhoon! The motion sickness was bad enough that they thought Jack had no "sea – legs" and maybe needed to be reassigned to a shore job.

After five days of sleeplessness, vomiting and clinging to the sides of his bunk, he recovered from the motion sickness and got used to walking with a zigzag swagger when at sea.

Although the ship had a surface to air missile system, anti-submarine surface launched and also rocket launched torpedoes, it had two automatic 5" rapid fire gun systems. Of all the functions the ship performed, none were as noticeable to the crew as firing the guns which rattled and shook everything aboard. A missile launch or ASROC (rocket launched torpedo) firing was almost un-noticeable, but fire the guns, everyone felt each round. The entire crew knew who he was and showed a degree of respect. A nickname he earned from the crew was "Jack Flash" or "The Flasher", primarily for the hypertensive attention to detail while on Bridge Watch. He became fond of the nick-name and found it an easy reference later for use in various motorsports endeavors.

He didn't like the Captain asking any questions for

which he didn't have a complete answer. Perhaps he perceived Jack as cocky, but after the first time he got "dressed-down" for an inaccurate answer to one of his questions, Jack made doubly sure he delivered full and complete status reports.

The ship made a few port visits to Taiwan, South Korea and Hong Kong. Hong Kong was his favorite for music store shopping and discotheques. The sophisticated urban environment spawned the most luxurious and technically equipped dance clubs. He loved disco and was accomplished in the various forms of the Hustle. From the first night, Jack met a luscious French-Philippino gal who was the equal to his dance skills. Brenda, a slender brunette with high cheeks and full lips knew how to "cut-the-rug" on the dance floor. She wouldn't give him her phone number, but agreed to meet him at the same club the next evening. They met and danced the three consecutive nights until the ship left port.

On deck, he spotted the Chief Boatswains Mate Lashbrook leaning on the life lines of the starboard side main deck. The muscular man was smoking a cigarette and gazing upon the Hong Kong skyline as Jack approached. He offered Jack a cigarette.

"Thanks Chief," Jack said as the CPO held the lighter for Jack's cigarette.

"There's such sadness, gnashing of teeth, hearts breaking! It's hard to watch the crew … tearful good-byes at the pier, last minute hugs, blown kisses … all the loved ones left behind as we leave port and head back to our wives and families," he mused.

"Such is the love life of a sailor."

For some reason, the presence of the buoy made Jack relive these fleeting moments. He felt the need to play something a bit jazzier, "Take Five" came to mind …… composed by saxophonist, Dave Brubeck and recorded in New York in 1959. What's unusual about this popular Jazz tune is the timing is 5/4 … which is ¼ beat longer per measure than the standard 4/4. It choked him up many times because Jack just wasn't used to counting measures by five. So the metronomic tapping of his foot on the boat hull didn't have the typical downbeat of 4/4, just an endless tap...tap...tap...tap...tap without counting. He made the musical phrase longer by a ¼ beat …

"Baa dip datt dodily dodily doo"

BURRO BONE CANYON

D riving the dark green Jaguar XKE eastbound on Otay Mesa Road, Jack was feeling great and looking cool. It was a warm clear San Diego morning, typical for late-May, not a cloud in the sky. He checked himself in the rear view to admire the new Ray Ban aviator sunglasses he had just bought … *"You're a handsome stud!"* he said aloud to himself, thinking that the only thing missing from this picture is a hot girl in the passenger seat blowing kisses to him.

He could almost imagine her being the young Lieutenant he met this week, Tiffany Maguire. She worked in the 32nd Street Naval Station's Public Affairs Office. She checked into the little office at the head of the pier for servicing the ships berthed there. As the ship's Public Affairs Officer, Jack would routinely drop off "Hometown News Flashes" on his way about the shipyard. These were simple "Seaman Recruit Smith of Any town just returned from overseas deployment on board USS Watson participating in multi-national maritime exercises FLEETEX 13 near the coast of

Taiwan" kind of story that small rural papers liked to run about a local boy in an exotic destination. They had just returned from an extended Western Pacific '76/'77 deployment and he had a handful of these newspaper blurbs to plant. Tiffany was a total dolly, in fact, she looked a lot like Marilyn Jameson except in a uniform and without all the accessories. The slender strawberry-blond was tall, leggy and very fit. He could easily imagine her at a beach volley-ball net making a jump for the ball. On a whim, he invited her to join him for lunch aboard the ship. She accepted much to his surprise.

"We can complete this press order this afternoon." Tiffany said then turned to the enlisted female next to her, *"Petty Officer Quinn, I'm going to lunch."*

"Would you like to lunch aboard ship?" Jack inquired.

"Is it nearby?"

"Yeah, just a few yards down this pier."

"Alright, which ship?" She came from behind the service counter and they walked through the door leading to the wharf and big gray ships.

"DDG Watson, just moored this morning."

"So one of your jobs is Public Affairs Officer, what else do you do?"

"Gunnery Division"

Their long stroll down the pier to his ship at the end was a little strange. It seemed every guy on the pier and aboard the multitude of ships berthed either side were busy checking her out. If this were a construction site of non-military men, she'd be drawing a cacophony of wolf whistles and cat calls. But she wore an Officer's uniform with a hemline just below the knee the enlisted guys liked, but dared not show their appreciation.

"We've been out for 10 months," Jack continued, *"half of the crew just off-loaded on Leave this morning."*

"Why didn't you?"

"I'll be timing my Leave for my dad's retirement. He had a long career in advertising. So, the PAO job, sorta follows his path ... he had PAO duties in the Army Air Corps during WWII. "

"So, you're thinking of pursuing a similar career?"

"Maybe, depending on what's out there. I'll have more Hometown Press Releases to bring to your office, shortly" he mentioned.

"Well, okay, anyone in the pier office can help you. I spend a lot of time in the base Public Affairs Office."

As they neared the bow of the USS Watson, her eyes drifted past him to the forward 5" Gun mount.

"Oh! You guys are one of the most decorated destroyers in the Pacific!"

"Gee, does that make this lunch any more special?"

"No," she sniffed, *"I've lunched on ships before."*

He liked the peripheral view of her walking beside him. He was surprised that as she spoke, she used her hands in describing things. He found it engaging, but very much a male form of communicating. Not a "girly-girl" he thought. Tiffany had a little grittiness or maybe it was the uniform.

Now some of his crew noticed her.

Jack attempted to keep her distracted with small chit-chat conversation so she wouldn't be discomforted by the attention, but she was well aware of the commotion her presence created and ignored it. Onboard, a few other junior officers joined them in the wardroom and showed visible confusion as to how Jack was the lucky one to host her visit. Somewhere in the lightweight chattling, she let it drop that her father was the Submarine Base Commander Admiral Maguire. Jack tried to imagine what protocol would exist around her and her dad with a prospective suitor, military or not. It was a big turn-off.

Yeah, Tiffany could be sitting there, but ... so could a lot of other hot girls.

Thrusting his arm out the Jaguar's window to float his hand in the air stream, the warming air pushed his hand around like the airfoil of the plane. The Bee Gees "You Should Be Dancing" played. He found himself doing a seated Hustle to the rhythm. *There's usually good looking girls at the Crystal Palace Disco, maybe I will go there tonight,* he thought.

The E-Type Jag with its long hood sporting dual rows of louver vents separated by the raised center contour of the bonnet, covered headlights and small oval snout already made him feel like a pilot. The purring engine was mesmerizing as the car ate up the desert road.

Approaching the familiar sign, Brown Field Municipal Airport, he turned left toward the cluster of hangers and buildings surrounded by planes, his destination was at the center of them. The little square clapboard building was a WWII left over and in need of attention. Out front, three Cessna 150s were parked, waiting for students.

Inside, the familiar female receptionist was absent. The desk was cleared as if it were no longer occupied. Past the reception desk and into the little office behind, a radio announcer reported a ball game.

"Hello Rudy, I'm back!" he said to the back of the tall balding thin man standing next to a file cabinet in a cloud of cigarette smoke. The lanky fellow turned around. A cigarette hanging from his mouth and the eye glasses propped up on his forehead. A middle-aged man, wearing a sweat stained short sleeved cotton bowling shirt that was too big for him.

"Oh! ...Hey!" he said, "Everything's great! What's up?"

"Well I thought I'd get back on the program," he stammered, "you know ... get my pilots license."

"Yeah? Sure! Got your logbook? Let me take a look." He handed over the thin black booklet to him. "So ... You were waiting to go on a ship, right?"

"Yeah, that's right. I was on leave the last time you saw me in November. I had to catch a MAC flight outta San Francisco to the Philippines," Jack revealed, "It took 14-hours non-stop and then a 4-hour bus ride through the worst mountain roads to the Naval Base at Olongapo. I caught up with my ship just a couple of weeks before Christmas. We *just got back in last week and I'm here to get things going again. I want to hurry up and finish this off so I can get my license."*

In retrospect, it seemed like the last nine months on deployment to the typhoon-prone Western Pacific was a dream or a nightmare, and he couldn't decide which. After all the crossing back and forth over the South China Sea in rough conditions yielded strong symptoms of motion sickness .

"Yeah grab a seat while I take a look at this thing," the man said as he sat down at the desk.

On the wall behind the desk was a bent airplane propeller surrounded by a montage of taped and stapled photographs, certificates and aerial maps. Rudy pulled his glasses down to the bridge of his nose and puffed on his cigarette.

"Yeah ... so it's ahh ... so it's been 10 months here ... that now you're going to start goin' again ... and ahh ... you've got about 30 hours ... almost 30 hours ... here so, we'll have to start the filling in the blanks ... you know, I mean ... to get you up to your 40 hour requirement and cover everything for the written part. Probably do another cross-country flight and the book stuff for passing the test."

Rudy asked glancing up from the logbook, *"You want to go up today?"*

"Well yeah, if it's okay ... I mean, you know, if you got a plane available and its okay."

"No problem," Rudy said as he got up from the desk and walked over to a panel of keys, *"I got number ... ahhhh ... "* he pulled one of the sets of keys off the panel, *"Here's 5017U, the white Cessna 150 you were in before. I think it has enough gas ... only one other person used it this morning for a little taxi practice. Be sure to check it has at least three-quarters of the wing tanks full of fuel on the pre-flight. If it's low, we'll gas it or I'll give you a different plane."*

He went on, *"So to get back into the swing of things I want you to go and do some touch-n-go take-offs and landings,"* he paused, *"... go around about three or four times. Then, fly over the Burro Bone Canyon practice area to the north up there just north of the Lone Star Road and do some power-on stalls ... practice those and then come back and that should be about an hour or so. And when you come back in,"* Rudy said removing his glasses and squinting, *"... then we'll figure what the next steps we'll do for your Pilot's License. Okay?"*

Jack stepped out of the building and spotted the white little high-wing Cessna 150 with a long blue accent stripe on its side. The clipboard had a pre-flight checklist that was the mandatory first step and he could see Rudy peeking through the window. So, he took his time ... vertical and horizontal stabilizer, ailerons, propeller, tires and engine oil level. After pulling the wheel chocks, he climbed in, inserted the key, checked the fuel gauge to finish the pre-flight checklist, put on the headset and got radio clearance from the control tower, *"Cessna 5017 Uniform go-ahead."*

It occurred to him that the two-seat trainer was little more than a frame covered with beer can thin aluminum and could be repaired with the metal from a 12-pack of beer and a pop-rivet gun. The small air-cooled engine had a humming vibration and with the hollow wings and main body, it seemed to create standing airwaves in the cockpit.

Standing on the brakes, he ran-up the engine to 1,700 rpm and noted the prop blast on the rudder and elevator surfaces. After warming up the engine and taxiing down to the end of the runway, he throttled up ... heading to the East ... the airspeed climbed 45mph ... 60 mph ... then felt the lifting of the wings. As the little two-seater aircraft lifts off the ground, he could feel an imbalanced wheel vibration come to a stop. A tightness in his throat ... blood pulsing in his neck and temples as the elevation increased. He took a couple of deep breaths to chill and it worked. As instructed, all traffic looped to the north side of the airport because the Mexican border was just a mile and a half to the south.

He leveled the plane at 1,300 feet, backed the throttle to 96 mph airspeed, banked to the left headed north. Past the end of the airstrip, he reduced engine power, banked left again and started the descent. Lining up with the runway, he further reduced power and put the plane into a nose-high attitude while watching the ground rise to meet the wheels.

"Perfect!" He congratulated himself aloud.

The airport had two parallel East-West strips, one 3,200 foot and the other 8,000 foot. These runways reflect on the airport's history as a Naval Auxiliary Air Station. Commissioned and decommissioned consecutively in support of training pilots for the two World Wars and Korean War, iconic military aircraft like P-38 Lightning, Wildcats, Avengers, Hellcats and many more roared over these runways. In contrast, the little two-seat Cessna needed only 1,300 feet at most.

Following two more "perfect" landings, he took off this time and climbed past 2,500 feet. The air was much cooler flowing into the cockpit … at 3,200 feet; he reduced engine power and leveled off … airspeed at 100 mph. He banked again to the left for a northerly path to the practice area. The vacant arid terrain is rough and rocky with mostly brown vegetation accented with occasional green spots of hardy shrub or cactus.

Looking down, he felt the tightness in his throat again. It was the same tightness he felt whenever he was in a high building, cliff, bridge, whatever and stood too close to a window or ledge. Directly below was Lone Star Road.

Another road a few miles ahead demarked the southern edge of the desolate practice area. No place to make an emergency landing with exception of that rough winding dirt road that crossed it. On charts it was identified as Wiley Road, demarking the southern rim of Burro Bone Gulch, a deep dry-stream. A string of power poles run along Wiley Road just opposite the gulch. Up on the right, the eastern delineation of the triangular shaped practice area was Lower Otay Lake. The northern edge was visually clear by the 4-lane Olympic Parkway and densely populated housing tracts just beyond, a "no-fly" area.

A scan showed no other aircraft around. Just above Wiley Road, he pulled the nose up and watched the indicated airspeed gauge fall ... 70 mph ... 50 mph ...

"BEEP! BEEP! BEEP!" the loud stall warning alarm startled him ... although he's heard it before, this time it wasn't expected and brought on a panic attack. The tiny plane suddenly shudders ... indicating that the stall speed of 48 mph had been reached.

The engine spinning to no avail as the airspeed drops off to zero... the alarm still screaming its warning ... the Cessna's left wing drops first, then yaws in the same direction ... in an instant, the plane is nose down ... *"Awww Shit!"* he yelled out as the roll continued and the only view was straight down at the coarse terrain.

"BEEP! BEEP! BEEP!"

"NO!! NO!! NO!!"

He frantically pulled back on the W-shaped control in his hands. All the gauges were wildly moving, spinning and impossible to read ... aside from the dazzling visual display, he couldn't read anything ... nothing made sense.

"BEEP! BEEP! BEEP!"

Straining to see through sun glare of the plastic windshield and metallic glint off the spinning propeller at a ravine below ... his throat tightened to a choke-hold ... the air was instantly thick, hot and he couldn't breathe!

The ravine angled off to the right side ... then popped back up of the left ... and again and again, each time going faster.

"BEEP! BEEP! BEEP!"

The engine growl increasing as it spun faster and faster. The sound of air rushing past the windows, through the wing struts and wheel gear raises pitch into a deafening howl.

The sweat rivulets drip off his nose as the ravine zooms larger and larger.

"SHIT! SHIT! SSHHHHIIIITTT!" he screamed jerking and turning the controls to make something happen.

"BEEP! BEEP! BEEP!"

Nothing worked … in a final act of desperation, he stomped on the rudder pedals, first right, then left. Suddenly, the left wing came up. The wings flexed and creaked under the strain to accept the load of the fuselage. Airflow over the elevator surfaces raised the nose. In a crab-like move, the plane yawed back to flying attitude.

The ravine now looked like a canyon and the rim of it was at eye-level. The propeller resumed its bite on the air. The incessant stall alarm stopped. The gauges stopped spinning. Directly ahead were utility poles and power lines.

"TOO LOW!! TOO LOW!!"

Full throttle and pulling the controls back to make the Cessna climb was the only way out.

It worked. The plane continued to climb to 1,200 feet, when he leveled off and aimed for Brown Field.

The enormity of what happened just hit, *"What the Fuck! That's it! I'm through with this! I am NEVER, EVER getting into another one of these fucking things!"*

Desperately trying to calm himself down, he was able to begin breathing again. Shortly, back on the ground in front of the school hanger, he chocked the wheels and repeated *"NEVER EVER!"* with each step toward the flight school building.

Soaked in sweat, shaking, he told Rudy what happened. The man sat behind the desk staring, turning white, when the cigarette fell out of his mouth and he didn't move to catch it or pick it up.

Back on Otay Mesa Road, all Jack could think of was a Bacardi Rum and Coke. The moment of truth, that he had a fear of heights so strong he could not logically recall what he had practiced so many times. It was something he should have recognized and conquered before having to ultimately face. A valuable lesson he would need another lifetime.

Even though he was just Stayin' Alive, he didn't feel like dancing.

ANOTHER COCONUT ON THE BEACH

The last days of 1979 were passing so slowly. It was bad enough when they were busy, but when they're just sitting ... waiting ... in the heat just on the International nautical border. He supposed the good part was actually catching up on sleep. He did a lot of that lately.

His eyes gravitated to the small photograph of Samantha. They dated the few times he went back to Michigan on Leave. On a spring date in 1977, he borrowed his Dad's Lincoln. Samantha and he went to a couple of discotheques. It was apparent that she couldn't touch-dance. He was an avid fan of the Hustle disco moves and had them down. Despite nearly falling on the dance floor, she kept smiling and her eyes were glued to his.

That night, he brought her home and they made love in his bedroom.

In the morning, George walked into the bedroom and looked about the dresser top for his car keys. He did not notice Jack was not alone. Samantha stirred. Jack reached over and pressed her head back into the pillow as if she were asleep. George found the keys and turned to leave. Jack pretended to be asleep also. George saw them and stood there a moment, then left the room.

A moment after hearing the door latch click, she softly asked,*"Are we in trouble?"*

"I don't know. But, I should get you home before something happens."

Jack quickly dressed and went downstairs while Samantha got up. When Jack reached the bottom step, he heard his father's angry voice, *"And what is your name?"*

"Samantha"

"Well Samantha, this isn't acceptable. It's time for you to leave … and I don't want to see you here again!"

On the kitchen counter, Jack found his car keys and picked them up. Jack ushered her to the car and they left.

They barely spoke on the five minute ride to her house. Jack was thoroughly embarrassed and angry at his father. After all, he was almost 24 and wasn't going to put up with it. *"I'm very sorry … pay no attention to what just happened. We must have startled him and he reacted like I was still in high school."*

"Don't worry, Jack. I won't."

She reached over and placed her hand on his. It stayed there until they reached her dad's house.

"I want to see you later," he said.

She smiled at him and he knew this was no ordinary young woman.

They departed days later with each others' address. Her first letter included the picture and the wonderful scent of her perfume. Her monthly letters were of school, the Andrews twins and her Cocker Spaniel, Taffy. He eagerly awaited each one. The little Polaroid instant photo taped to his desk, was the only color in an otherwise grey closet of an officer stateroom that he shared with Henry, another junior officer. Her best friend, Sophia took the picture. A petite blond with a tom-boyish grin leaning against the back deck rail of the Andrew's house with a backdrop of late summer Michigan maple trees. She had long straight hair that went down to her tight little butt … a modern era Lady Godiva. She became the focal point of his daydreaming.

The door of the stateroom opened and hit the back of his chair. Jack shifted the chair to the right to give Henry room to squeeze in between him and the sink. *"So, what's the news? When are we moving again?"* Jack asked.

"It looks like we're going back to Diego Garcia maybe this afternoon," he murmured, *"I dunno, Captain is still deciding … he's got Ensign Anderson firing messages everywhere."*

"Just us again? Are the other ships just gonna sit out here?"

"Looks that way … Engineering is lighting up number two … got the boiler pipes patched … so …" Henry's shrug indicated it was all "maybe" stuff.

He pulled off his glasses and lay down on the lower bunk. It was easy to see the Combat Information Center was at full-tilt. Even at radio-silence, it was the hub of activity with the sonar boys listening for Russian subs, EW guys listening to any traffic or targeting emissions, radar techs staring at screen sweeps looking for missiles and aircraft. Jack was glad he wasn't up there. In that darkened room, all the info flowed and got instantly recorded by grease pencil on clear lexan grids with the Captain, Executive Officer and or Operations Officer sitting in the middle nervously studying and waiting.

What started out as a multi-nation naval exercise in the Indian Ocean, Operation MIDLINK with Australian, British, Pakistani and Iranian fleets, turned into Arabian Sea MODLOC. The whole thing unraveled when the Iranian ships made an unannounced departure and headed homeward in response to the Iranian Revolution with the overthrow of the Shah Pahlavi dynasty. Next to go were the Brits and Pakistanis. Then with no cool stuff to do, the aircraft carrier went back to the Pacific.

All the ship's planned ports-of-call got chopped ... leaving them and the Aussies to make just one visit to the port of Karachi, Pakistan ... and then sit at a spot in the ocean,"MODLOC", for months at a time in "contingency" status with possible American citizen rescue from Iran. Christmas and New Year's, needless to say, were depressing.

On the deck of the ship, one could look north and see atmospheric clouds of terrestrial dust forming. Eventually, these clouds drifted south and dropped on them at night. It was hot, too. Some of the crew, sunbathing on the anti-submarine rocket launcher "ASROC" deck. The crew nick-named the area "the beach", as so much dust settled there. The dust got into the ships cooling systems and clogged filters for crew and electronic air conditioning inlets. Even the surface of the water surrounding the ship had layers of dust. Without any wind or sea influence, the ship just sat in the exact location day after day even though they were not anchored. The galley crew often threw punctured and weighted bags of refuse overboard, but they did not sink. Eventually, the ship was ringed by its own garbage. Gunners' mates were called out to target practice and shoot the floating garbage bags in an attempt to sink them. Some of it worked ... and some of it simply made the garbage patch larger as the bags tore open and the debris spread out.

So, the good news was they're returning to Diego Garcia, a coral atoll just south of the equator in the central Indian Ocean! Whoopee!

This British/U.S. military installation was uninhabited until the late 18th century when European overseers developed the dry land rim as a coconut plantation and imported contract workers of African, Indian and Polynesian descent. It is a horse-shoe shaped island, about fifteen miles long and four miles wide, and forms a nearly complete rim of land around a lagoon. About 90% of its perimeter is enclosed with an opening only in the north. Initial U.S. use was as a Naval Communications Station, and then Seabees built an airfield and hangers.

With the Iranian problem that popped up, someone in Washington decided that the surface NAVY would need a more prominent presence in the Indian Ocean. So, the ship was dispatched to evaluate the atoll as a future NAVY combatant ship harbor. Preliminary evaluation of the atoll indicated that the lagoon itself was deep enough and the channel marginally navigable. The objective was to enter the lagoon, anchor and be the "test pig" for the Seabees possible marina project until now, only small craft have done so.

Approaching Diego Garcia, Jack stood on the signal deck just above the pilot house. He marveled at the transparency of its crystal clear waters and the aqua / turquoise colors of its surrounding corals. Once inside the lagoon, Jack's station was at the ship's bow with the deck crew ready to drop anchor.

Navigating the channel was very slow ... it proved to be both narrow and shallow. It was obvious the Seabees would have to dynamite a better channel as this destroyer is one of the smaller surface ships to make harbor. They launched the motor-whale boat and Captains Gig just before dropping the anchor. After monitoring the ships position awhile, it was apparent that the anchor didn't "set" due to the hard coral bottom of the lagoon and with a moderate wind, dragged anchor. It was remedied by veering more chain, but it was not an adequate long-term fix. The Seabees would also have to install mooring buoys affixed to the lagoon bottom for a future as a Naval Support Facility.

Now that they had spent a few months at MODLOC, this time in the Gulf of Aden on "contingency operations", the news of returning to Diego Garcia was welcomed! Even though the U.S. side of the island had one thousand five hundred Seabees, none of which were female, the crew would be granted "shore leave" for a little R & R. Scuttlebutt word quickly got around that they'd have an interdivisional softball game, complete with barbeque and beer!

During the short transit from MODLOC to the atoll, the crew split into softball teams. Rivalries formed during the two day transit and some betting may have taken place as well. Jack had some notions about snorkeling in the lagoon. Others had cash in pocket and were ready to hit the PX for food, souvenirs music, reading material or anything else that might make shipboard life more comfortable.

Jack watched the process of pulling cases of Budweiser from a lockup below and loading it all in to the motor whale boat. Chief Boatswains mate, Lashbrook, was assigned to escort the suds to the ball field and "supervise" ice-down. The two were standing next to the Tartar Missile launcher.

"Big day, Chief," Jack said, *"We've got an excited crew just itching to get ashore."*

"Yeah, they're not the only ones," the muscular man

snorted gesturing at the Captain's Gig headed to the pier. They both knew the new Captain, a rotund little man with a heavy southern accent, would get well lubed while here and in Jackal-Hyde like fashion, turn into a swell guy. Then upon leaving port, it would take a few days to dry-out during which he became the other one.

Just then, Jack saw some black tipped reef sharks swimming about the ship. *"Wow, look at them all,"* he said pointing at what must have been a school of them.

"Oh, yeah! This place is infested with sharks. No one's allowed to go swimming."

"What?"

"Too many sailors have been bitten, so now nobody is allowed to go in the water for any reason," he said, *"and they used to have little sailboats and row boats for fishing … had to chop those all up too."*

"Ehhh, so that means no snorkeling or diving?"

"Yes, sir."

Jack swallowed his words and almost choked on them when a large gray object approached the ship from the stern. He pointed. They watched as it drew closer.

"A hammerhead!" Jack blurted upon making out the "T" shaped head approaching the starboard quarter.

One of the deckhands loading the Budweiser into the boat alongside noticed and called out to the coxswain in the boat, "Hey, Larry! Look ..."

"Mother-Fucker!"

"Oh, Shit!" All eyes were on the shark swimming up the starboard side. As the shark momentarily lined up next to the twenty-six foot motor whale boat, it was easy to see it was a few feet longer! The crew commotion caught the attention of the First Class Quartermaster up on the ships bridge-wing who peered at it swimming by.

"Keep an eye on these guys, Chief," Jack said as he turned and headed toward the bridge.

Once in the pilothouse, the First Class Petty Officer looked up and said, *"That's Hector."*

"Hector?"

"The Chief Warrant Officer who came out to help pilot us through the channel told us that Hector was the first inhabitant of the island and it was his lagoon," he said. *"He also told us to expect Hector will be lying over the top of our anchor when we pull up to leave. It's just something he does."*

"I'll be damned! Has he ever eaten anyone?" Jack inquired, to which he got an "I don't know" shrug.

"Looks like Chief Lashbrook should know this." Jack left the bridge to return to the boat alongside.

The rest of the Budweiser got loaded onto the boat and departed with the Chief. Crew in civvies with softball gear got shuttled to shore. Jack waited a couple of hours until he knew the beer would be cold and food already served. He had a few more leisure moments alone with Samantha's image before changing clothes and leaving. Just as the sun neared the horizon to set, Jack went ashore and was the only passenger the coxswain ferried.

Motoring to beach, the warm gentle breeze felt good. The western sky was coloring pink and the last of the sun cast long orange rays. It was such a beautiful place. In the distance there was shouting. Figuring it was the game underway, Jack headed in that direction along a footpath between the palm trees and ferns. He encountered a few of the crew heading in the opposite direction. He pointed in the direction of the shouting where he was headed and received a nod in response.

As he drew closer to the field, more yelling, but this sounded angrier. The light was growing dim and he could make out a clearing ahead and could see the smoke rising from the barbeque and it smelled great.

As he approached the fellow at the grill, he asked, *"What's going on here?"*

"A fight broke out, Mr. Springer. The Master-at-Arms and Shore Patrol are on it."

"Okay. I'll take two burgers and a dog. That's too bad … Damn!"

Jack prepped his food with condiments at the adjoining table and grabbed a beer from the iced barrel of Bud.

"Do you want anything else, Mr. Springer? We're gonna start packing up."

"No thanks, I'm good."

After choking down the food, Jack went back to the barrel of beer and found a whole six-pack. He would find somewhere away from this mess to consume the beer as the prospect of sitting in a beach hut watching the ship's officers lube-up was the last thing he wanted to do. It was dark now and the residual glow in the western sky didn't offer help in finding the path. With the glow behind him, he left the clearing onto another footpath through the palms. It led him to a small beach inside the lagoon. A downed palm tree trunk lay on its side in the white coral sand at the edge of the undergrowth. He sat down and popped one open.

From here, he could see most of the lagoon and monitor the ship. The motor whale boat ferried drunken crewmen back to the ship, their boisterous voices carried on the water. The eastern sky was already dark but revealing a density of stars he had never seen. The moon was very bright and illuminated almost like the sun. Another beer and thinking about Samantha's photo on his desk.

"This is paradise!" he caught himself saying, *"... and I'm alone without you."*

He wondered what she was doing ... maybe having lunch with some college classmates in the Student Union. Another beer and he laid himself out on the fine, soft, white sand with his head propped up on the palm log like a pillow. The soft sounds of a light breeze through the palm leaves overhead, the lapping of the lagoon water on the sand, a cricket-like clicking and a distant rustling of the undergrowth.

"Oh, if you were here right now!" he mumbled before popping the next can, *"... this is paradise! Well ... except for Hector!"*

The ferrying of crew slowed considerably, but the Captain's Gig would stay late. He had plenty of time ...

He dozed a little ... finished a beer, then popped open the last one. He took another long swig and stared at the star band of equatorial night sky. She can't be here to experience this, so he'll have to write her about it. It was the only thing he could think of doing to share this moment. He dozed a bit more … amazed there weren't any biting mosquitoes or flies … but there must be crickets, the clicking sound was closer.

"Gol-dang! There must be ants!" he mused as his scalp had a tickling sensation.

The rustling sound and clicking noise was right behind his head. He bolted upright and dusted his hair. Now the clicking noise was faster and right behind. Movement in the corner of his eye!

Now to his feet, he turned around to look at the huge dark spider where his head had just been. Jumping back, almost falling, he stared as the creature advanced over the palm trunk to where his shoulders had been and stopped. Probably two feet wide and a half foot tall, it raised its massive claws and clicked like a machine gun.

Transfixed in his sight, it crawled sideways back over the palm trunk and into the ferns.

"What the fuck is that?" he said aloud, rubbing his eyes scanning about for others. The clicking stopped, but there was more rustling in the undergrowth. All the beer he drank was now

pushing. He took few steps toward the water and he ripped a four foot stream.

Rounding up the cans and forcing them into the six-pack plastic collars, he didn't see anything moving and followed the beach back to the boat landing. The Coxswain sat at the dock next to the Captain's Gig chatting with someone as he waited for the officers.

Recognizing Jack, the Coxswain got to his feet, *"Ready to go back, Mr. Springer?"*

"In a moment Larry."

I'll take those cans for you, sir," Larry's companion said.

"I just had the shit scared out of me!" handing him the refuse, *"down there on the beach … this giant spider …"* he gestured.

"Coconut crabs, sir. This place is infested with them! They come out at night to feed."

"God Damn!"

"We don't go out without a flashlight … shine the light on them and they leave you alone."

"Didn't have one!"

"Those things will really hurt if they get a hold of you ... strong enough to open coconuts. You really need a flashlight ... shine the light under them and they'll release."

Larry started the Captain's Gig engine, "Climb aboard, Mr. Springer."

Back in his bunk ... he slept like a log ...

The next day, he went back ashore and found himself in a waiting line to get into the base store. The shelves were bare of most snacks and food items. There were still some radios and t-shirts with phrases about choking chickens ... not much else. Jack next headed over to the beach bar ... a Bloody-Mary sounded like a good idea ... unfortunately, they were just about wiped out of most everything thanks to the ship's wardroom of thirsty officers.

On the way back to the boat landing, Jack took a different route, almost every Seabee hut had the big crabs sitting on wooden blocks, cans, etc. some were in poses as if attacking, some were stretched out to be flat, and others were drinking out of a bottle or smoking a pipe or cigar. Some had a glossy lacquer, but many did not. Jack engaged a fellow sitting nearby reading a Stars and Stripes.

"Good Morning! May I interrupt you a moment?"

"Yeah, sure. Are you off that ship?"

"Yes, I am."

"There are a lot of guys here who are pissed at you!"

"Really? How come?"

"You guys wiped out our store and we won't get resupplied for weeks. That's the only thing we have out here!"

"Gee, I'm sorry for that. We've been in your same situation on that ship the last coupla months," he responded. "Say, what's with the crabs?"

"Coconut Crabs, this place is infested with them … like hundreds per acre. Nocturnal feeders … They live underground during the daytime and come out at night to climb palm trees for the coconuts, which they eat. The guys stationed here get bored, so they go out at night and catch them as souvenirs to take home."

He bent down to examine the massive front claws on the dead crab. "Anybody lose a finger?"

"Hell, yes! Those big claws can tear open coconuts, but they eat almost anything … rats, birds, fruit … even each other. They sometimes will jump off the *trees and once the claws lock-on to something; it's really hard to get them to release their grip. We get the Corpsman to inject them with formaldehyde to kill and then position them,"* he went on, *"rigor mortis sets in and they stay in position until they completely dry out. Then, when they stop stinkin', they get lacquered."*

Jack shook his head in disbelief.

"Yeah, the base commander wants it to stop but hasn't formally announced it, so that's why you see so many of them now ... it's been our last chance to get one while we still can. And these guys will be rotating outta here soon. The replacements won't be able to hunt them."

As he walked back to the boat landing, he wondered if his head looked like a coconut on that fallen palm trunk last night.

HAWAII FIVE-OH!

The past week could have been a simple transit. The crew was burned out from this deployment and anxious to get home. The flotilla command decided to continue the war games. For the Operations and Weapons groups aboard, it meant catching a couple hours of sleep whenever one could. The operations had the ships chasing ghost submarines, intercepting enemy aircraft, engaging surface threats and maneuvering into just about all of the sector screening and zigzagging in the books. With the exception of the full-ship General Quarters Alarm with the PA shrill Bos'n Pipe *"All Hands Man Your Battle Stations"*, the Engineering and Supply groups had regular watch rotations.

It was May 9th, 1979 and Jack had the 4am-8am Officer of the Deck watch on the Bridge. All was quiet. The Junior Officer of the Deck, Ensign Enrique Velez, was monitoring a surface radar contact.

"Whatcha got?" Jack asked him.

"*Big surface contact in the shipping lane … but he'll pass astern a few miles out.*"

Jack stepped out onto the portside bridge wing and gazed at the full moon and the shimmering highway of silver on the waters' surface. He stuck his head inside the bridge.

"*Quartermaster, what time does this moon set?*"

"*A few minutes just after sunrise at 5:57, sir. They should both be up and touching the horizon at the same time. We should have a great view … low humidity, clear sky. Technically, it's called 'Selenelion', but the sailors of old called it the 'Kings Treasure'*" he quipped, "*it's the simultaneous moon set and sunrise 180-degrees apart.*"

Enrique stepped out to the bridge wing as the Quartermaster exited and said, "*I've heard about the 'Kings Treasure'. That's when the sun and moon are on opposite horizons at the exact same time and look like gold and silver coins.*"

"*I haven't seen it either,*" Jack responded, "*… but if seeing it meant losing another minute of rack time …*"

"*I hear ya,*" Enrique said with a scowl. He pulled a cigarette out of a pack and offered them to Jack. He accepted one and he extended his lit flip-top Zippo, then lit his own.

"Thanks," Jack said. The nicotine helped to stimulate the sleep-deprived much like the rancid coffee that was always available while on watch. *"Four hours of sleep a day ... sucks!"*

Jack stuck his head inside the bridge wing door. The Quartermaster was updating the ships position based on the SATNAV coordinates just reported. Like an artist, he drew a precise little "X" on the navigational chart of the Hawaiian island waters with a freshly sharpened pencil point.

"Quartermaster, when you can, please step out here."

"Yes, sir."

A moment later, the fellow stepped out to the bridge wing. Enrique was looking for his radar contact with binoculars they were obligated to wear while on watch.

"Sir?"

"How are we tracking?" Jack asked.

"Very good, Mr. Springer, we're tracking right on the DR line to the mouth of Pearl Harbor."

"Good! " he responded, *"Have you been briefed on our entry into Pearl?"*

"Yes, sir, we are to be the first ship in at about ten this morning. We'll be ahead of the Cruiser STRAPPED and Frigate BENDOVER and proceed to the Ammunition Depot for offload. Sometime this afternoon, we'll be moving to the Makalapa Bravo pier for crew departure and early Tiger boarding."

Enrique and Jack locked eyes.

"And the Navigation Detail will be set when?" Jack asked.

"Expecting 9 am, depending … "

In the moon's luminescence, Jack could see Enrique's eyes roll.

"Great! Great! That'll be all, thanks."

"Yes, sir." The quartermaster disappeared.

"Well, Enrique, wanna take a bet the Captain sets the Navigation Detail when we get off watch?"

"Bastard! No sleep … and no chow!" he whispered, *"He probably would, too!"*

Enrique went back inside the bridge while Jack lingered gazing at the moon and its reflection. It was beautiful, and he could understand the seafaring man's impression of wealth.

In awhile, the eastern horizon brightened and revealed the silhouette of Oahu off the starboard bow.

"Mr. Springer," the quartermaster called to Jack as he crossed the bridge to the starboard wing, *"Sunrise in five."*

"Got it, thanks."

Sure enough, the golden orb broke the surface with a ray that lit up the peaks of the oceans swells as if a Leprechaun were flying about overhead dropping gold coins on the ocean's surface.

Enrique stepped out onto the starboard bridge wing to watch.

"God Bless! Look at that!" he exclaimed, as they watched the gold grow into a bright solid band on the water's surface.

Inside the bridge, the quartermaster was telling the helmsman and lee helmsman about the solar-lunar event taking place. He spotted Jack seeing him and abruptly stepped away, as it's an offense to distract the watch crew from their duties.

Jack stepped into the bridge, *"Okay boys, check it out!"*

Everyone on watch was alternatively looking from port to starboard to see the 'Kings Treasure'. For about a minute, both sun and moon touched opposite horizons. The big coins just touched their respective shimmering highways to converge upon the ship. Silver on the portside and gold on the starboard side … and for those few fleeting seconds, the experience made Jack feel like they were the richest men on earth!

The next hour and a half quickly passed in a daydream about Samantha's photo on his desk.

"Captain's on the bridge!" the Quartermaster announced with the sudden presence of the rotund, disheveled captain.

*"Officer of the Deck! Tell me what's going on, "*he commanded.

Jack promptly approached and pointed out the presence of the other naval ships, commercial traffic, the ship's present course, speed and navigation position relative to Pearl Harbor.

The Signalman on watch entered the starboard bridge wing door and handed Jack the flashing light message of the Commodore's next maneuver to the Task Group. He informed the Captain.

"Lieutenant Springer, when the Commodore

executes that order, I want the Navigation Detail established."

"Aye, aye, Captain!"

Sure enough, the Commodore executed the order, and Jack ordered the Boatswain Mate of the Watch to pipe reveille over the PA and announce the setting of the new watch. Navigation Detail is called anytime the ship operates in restricted waters that may imperil the ship like reefs, ports, and channels. The entire crew is in a state of readiness.

Some hours later, inside Pearl Harbor, the ship off-loaded most of the ammunition.

A small number of the five inch projectiles and enough powder charges to fire the ships two guns in demonstrations for the civilian guests, the "Tigers."

Once the offload was completed and gun magazines emptied, the ship was moved with tug boats to the Makalapa Bravo Pier.

Here, about twenty percent of the crew debarked on leave. Most of them climbed aboard waiting busses to transport them to Ohana Honolulu Airport and flights back to the mainland. The berthing vacancies were needed for "Tigers", the male family members of the crew who were to ride aboard the ship for the week-long transit to San Diego.

A short time later, Jack was at the base gate and out of uniform when he heard his name called. *"Lieutenant Springer!"* the big voice bellowed.

Without turning he knew it was his Dad. There he was waving, *"Lieutenant!"*

Never shy, the tall ruddy faced man with white hair standing next to a brand new town car liked the attention he drew from the cluster of others waiting. In the passenger seat of the pale yellow car, a sandy brown haired boy squinted through a window.

"Hey, Big D!" Jack called back, *"Is that Garrett?"*

"Hi Uncle Jack," the 12 year old replied, *"It's me!"*

After bear-hugging the old man, Jack climbed into the back seat and mussed his nephew's mop of hair from behind.

"What a surprise!" Jack exclaimed, *"Great to see you, Gare!"*

"We got in this morning and did a little sight-seeing after checking into the hotel," George said as he hung a right on Kamehameha Highway.

"*Nice wheels. You two are travelling in style,*" Jack said as they passed the Ohana Airport exit.

"*A loaner from our local agency office,*" George explained, "*… a product placement car for the television show 'Hawaii 5-0'. Even after retiring, I still have a little pull.*"

"*Book 'em Daddy-O!*" Jack quipped.

"*Say, we haven't eaten. Are you hungry?*"

"*Oh, man! I'm beat,*" he said, "*… didn't get bit of sleep last night. I'm really dead, but I'm hungry as anything for some real food.*"

"*Well, we can take care of that right away Lieutenant … get some NAVY grog in you and … fix you right up!,*" George said winking through the rear view mirror. A moment later, they were in the parking lot of a tacky tourist restaurant called Wicki Wacki Bob's Bar & Grill.

Jack squeezed Garrett's shoulders, "*Are you having fun with Gramps?*"

"*Yeah,*" the boy murmured, "*… it's okay.*"

They were ushered to a booth in the tropically themed 'Shipwreck' section. After a few minutes study of Bob's menu, a couple of NAVY Grog's appeared. George wasn't one to waste time when libations were concerned.

The punch tasted really good and went down fast ... a couple more ordered with their meal. With each round, George would say "Cheers!" with a wink. Jack cleared his plate and had still had room for more.

"We've been looking forward to this week ... should be a lotta fun ... and maybe learn something about what you've been doing on the ship," he said eyeing his grandson.

"Yep! It'll be a real pant-load alright. All kinds of activities are planned ... firing a missile, shooting the guns, we'll refuel alongside a supply ship ... and meet some of the characters I have to deal with," Jack said with a smirk on his face.

He could tell his dad wanted to have a 'man-chat' by the way he rolled his eyes to the boy and gave a nod.

"I ... ahhh need to take you to the Officer's Club for a 'Security Briefing', Dad" Jack lied with a wink, *"but ... ahhh, youngsters aren't allowed in there, so ...."*

"Oh? That's too bad," George smiled, *"but Garrett's a big guy and will be responsible enough for just a couple of hours alone at the hotel ... right, Gare?"*

"Yeah, I can watch television."

Lubed up and feeling pretty good, Jack and father left Wiki Waki Bob's and were back in the 'Hawaii 5-0' town car. George drove the big car in a sporting fashion and had them at an airport hotel in minutes. Jack waited in the car, while George took Garrett into the hotel and, no doubt, left instructions that they'd be back shortly.

Jack dozed a little due to the lack of sleep until a boisterous *"Okay, Lieutenant! Where to?"*

"How about the Royal Hawaiian?"

"Just what I was thinking!" he said.

It was a short drive to the Royal Hawaiian, an old iconic pink colored hotel on Waikiki Beach that was their family vacation spot more than a decade ago. He parked the car on Don Ho Street to avoid using the hotel's valet. They walked through the large lobby full of lush flowers and immaculately manicured grounds past the swimming pool and down to the beach bar.

It was warm and the sun was starting to set. They sat at the bar, toes in sand and in view of Diamond Head. As if by magic, a pair of NAVY Grog's appeared!

"*Cheers,*" George said, "*and we're halfway around the world since the last time we were able to do this.*" Jack knew he was referring to the African Safari trip they made in celebration of his college graduation. There was a strong likeliness of the Royal Hawaiian Beach Bar hut with its pole frame and thatched roof to many of the African structures they experienced.

"*Now that,*" Jack said, "*was an adventure I'll never forget! And I've got you to thank for it.*"

"*I ran into Bill Jameson not long ago,*" George said, "*His two daughters had a terrible time in Scotland and Ireland. It was cold and raining the whole time. They wish they stayed in Amsterdam.*"

"*Yes, that would have been interesting,*" Jack admitted.

The still warm air was broken by a light breeze coming off the water. It made the glow from the tiki-torches gently wave inside the thatched roof hut and transformed his father's face into the young man he once was.

"*I've got to tell you, dad, I've been thinking long and hard about this whole NAVY thing. I'm not seeing my future in it. I got a year to go ...*"

"*Oh? I thought you liked it.*"

"Ehhh! Most of the junior officers have troubles at home ... long absences at sea, wives struggling as single parent, extra-marital shit happening, divorces, money problems ... might be okay for a single guy wanting to stay that way ... but that's just part of it. I don't get enough sleep, don't make enough money, and don't get to see much beyond the boozing and whoring in the ports."

"Yeah? Well, maybe that's for the better. Service is a good resume builder anyway," George said.

"This one time, we were playing war games in the South China Sea, and I was standing in the main passageway with all the senior officers of the ship ... the Captain totally lost it and was screaming at the Executive Officer who turned and screamed at the rest of us. There was plenty of heartburn to pass around! I decided right then and there, that I didn't look forward to that as my future."

Time passed and more Grog appeared ... Jack had a confession to make.

"I have to tell you something ... by the way ... I thought about it recently."

"Oh, yeah? What's that?"

"Well ... when I was about six in Garden City ... I was playing gas station attendant in the garage ...

and you had new car in there ... I walked up to the driver's window and I said "Yes sir! Filler Up?" ... an "Want me to check under the hood?" ... an stuff like that. So ... I walked around to the other side of the car and took the garden hose off the holder ... an walked around the car ... took the gas cap off an put the hose in ... an turned on the faucet to fill it up! *When it was full, I turned off the faucet, returned the hose and put the gas cap back on. I went to the driver's window and said "She's full up, sir! Anything else I can do for you?" ... an then the customer said "No, thank you very much!" ... and she drove away."*

His dad's face turned from astonished to hilarious, *"That was you? Ha! Ha! Ha! Ha! Ha!"* he laughed hard enough to tear his eyes and then smacked the bar top. *"Ho! Ho! Ho! Ho!"* shaking his head back and forth, *"No! I didn't know that!"*

"Yes! I remember it now! One day I drove to work and the car just quit. A few miles from home it just stopped. It wouldn't start again, so I had it towed to the dealership. They went through everything! Couldn't find out what was wrong! Just by luck, a mechanic smelled his fingers and didn't smell gas. I got the call later and they said I must have gotten some bad gas somewhere because there was a lot of water in the gas tank! HA! HA! HA! HA! So that was you! That clears up a great big mystery I've pondered for years!"

Suddenly relieved he took it so well, Jack admitted, *"Yeah! Ha ha ha! Sorry about that! I wasn't ever going to tell you. But I thought of it just now."*

George put his arm around his son's shoulders, *"That's funny! The things we do as kids ... Say, how about one more for the road, Lieutenant?"*

"Oh boy, okay! I'm gonna sleep pretty hard tonight."

The bartender brought up a couple more NAVY Grogs. The dark Myers rum floater on top tasted great and it went down with ease.

But standing up off the bar stools, Jack knew they were both feeling the drinks' impact. He could barely walk through the lobby without bumping into stuff.

Back at the car, George tossed Jack the keys, *"You know your way around here ..."*

Well he didn't. Downtown Honolulu was comprised of a bunch of one-way streets and a lagoon in the middle of it all. So the instant Jack put the big car into 'Drive', they were lost.

"We gotta get back on the freeway" he said.

All the windows down in the balmy night air didn't help to snap the dozy feeling. Everything was a comfortable and colorful blur ... even the street girls ... he made a right-hand turn and started up the hill ... to the highway ramp ... entry ramp ... but wasn't there ... kept on driving up hill ... to a circular drive in front of a large building ... hospital?

"We're going the wrong way ..."

"I'll turn around in this drive," Jack said, turning right.

"Wait ... STOP!"

"What?"

BANG! They hit something ... got out of the car ... the front was a little higher but looked okay.

*"Didn't you see the pole?"*George asked, referring to steel pipes arranged to block off the street.

"No"

"That thing is bent over and hooked behind the bumper ... Oh, boy ... we're not getting outta here without a wrecker." George looked at Jack and gestured toward the lit-up building, *"Why don't you go on in there and see if you can get us a wrecker."*

Jack stumbled up to the lit building ... a library full of students ... He asked someone sitting at a front desk

to call a wrecker because of an accident outside …
everyone was staring at him … was he too loud? …
back outside, George was pacing around the front
of the car … he waves Jack back … to go back …
all these people followed him out of the building!
George did not want the growing assemblage of
students to alert the authorities.

Ever the creative quick thinker, George ran toward
the growing cluster of curious onlookers and waved
his arms to back up, *"GET BACK! MOVE BACK
INSIDE! WE'RE SHOOTING SCENES FOR 'HAWAII
FIVE-OH' TELEVISION SHOW! GET BACK!"*

*"There's the prop car and two actors, but no
cameras,"* someone in the crowd said, while others
looked around for the camera crew.

George rushed over to Jack, *"Let's get them away!
We don't need the attention!"* He waved to them
to go and shouted, *"YOU'RE RUINING OUR SHOOT!
BACK UP! GO BACK INSIDE!"*

Nobody moved … campus security pulled up
… more flashing lights … police radio chatter …
wrecker … people talking and laughing … George
talking to a cop … then it was quiet and everyone
was gone … and Jack was alone sitting on the curb.

Have to go back to the ship … walking down the hill
… across a bridge … up a street … another bridge …

up a hill ... somebody laughing ... these ferns and thick underbrush ... sweet smell ... tangled up in vines ... not like a Philippines jungle ... Vietnam! ... a jungle he couldn't get through!

More laughing ...he recognized the voices and followed them to a clearing ... laughing ... bastards from the USS CONGRESSIONAL aircraft carrier ... muffled conversations from inside the building ... damn A-7 pilots! ... pranksters and practical jokers ... I'm on to them now!

Muffled talk ... more laughing ... banging on the door ... won't let me in ...

Jack woke with a start. Someone's kicking his feet.

"Come On! Wake Up!" A booming voice said, *"Wake Up! Open Your Eyes!"*

Blindingly bright, Jack raised his arm to shield his eyes and squinted at the man kicking his feet. He wore a badge.

"Do you know where you are?"

"No"

"Okay, let's get up!"

He could make out that the man wore a blue

uniform. Jack rolled to his right to get up to a sitting position.

"Oh, man! I must have had too much to drink last night."

He sat for a moment. There was something dark on the floor along his left side. The policeman patiently waited as Jack steadied himself.

There was someone on the floor next to him!

"Do you have some identification?"

The person lying next to him sat up and stared him in the eyes. Crisp white linen surrounded a pleasant but plain face in a habit ... a nun! She said nothing.

Jack felt a burst of energy to stand up.

"Yes, sir" he stammered. He put his military ID in the officer's outstretched hand.

"Okay Lieutenant, what happened?"

They were standing in the back of a school classroom with kid-size desks. Jack rubbed his pounding head to think ... last night ...

"I drank too much ... I thought I was in Vietnam and this is where the A-7 pilots were bunking."

The officer gestured to look behind. *"You realize you broke a window?"*

"No, sir" he turned to see a brick and broken glass on the floor next to a door.

"Okay, come with me," he said and gestured to the open door on the other side of the room.

Blinded by the rising sun as they exited the building, the officer motioned for him to use the handrail going down the courtyard steps. In the center of the courtyard, another police officer was taking notes and talking with a heavyset nun and man in work clothes.

"Wait here." Jack looked back in the classroom but the nun who was lying on the floor next to him had gotten up and left.

The officer walked over to the others ... a brief discussion took place. He returned and handed Jack the Navy ID card.

"Do you have any donation you can make to the school for the broken window?"

Jack opened his wallet and handed over the only cash he had, two twenty dollar bills. *"Okay, I'll be right back."*

The officer joined the others … more discussion … then returned.

"Okay Lieutenant, let's get you out of here."

Once inside the squad car, he said *"I'll drop you off at a taxi stand up ahead. You'll have to pay him once he gets you back on base."*

"Oh! Thank you so much! My ship will be pulling out soon and if I miss it … BIG TROUBLE!"

"It's a little past six, I'll take you as far as I can." He flipped on the siren and lights to rip down the hillside.

He drove Jack down to a liquor store where two taxicabs sat. He got out, walked over and talked to the first driver. He gestured for Jack to get out of the squad car and into the cab.

"This guy will take you back as quickly as he can. He knows to wait at the ship for you to retrieve money to pay him. Good Luck, Lieutenant. Be more careful with the drinking."

Jack thanked the officer again. The cabbie took off like a shot and drove faster than the officer had. His head was pounding. It hurt to even keep his eyes open. He just hung on. They raced into the NAVY compound and up the pier tires squealing. ID in hand

Jack sprinted up the gangway and to his safe in his stateroom. The cab driver didn't charge him as much, but Jack felt it was the best sixty bucks he ever spent!

Back in his stateroom, he flopped on the bunk. His reeling booze-soaked brain trying to figure out what happened and what he had to do next, when there was a banging on the door. It was Chief Lashbrook, *"Mr. Springer! We don't have all the Tigers on board and I've been looking all over for you."*

"Oh man! I tied one on last night … I can't believe it! I don't know where my dad and nephew are … they should be coming along anytime … How much time before getting underway?"

"I think we've got about 45 minutes before we start pulling lines up. I think you better change into uniform."

Chief Lashbrook closed the door and left. Jack took a long shower … things improved slightly.

"Mr. Springer," Petty Officer Jones said, *"we're starting to make preps to get underway. Chief Lashbrook and I got you covered."*

"Okay, thanks!"

Jack hung on to the main deck lifeline as he watched the quarterdeck get dismantled in preparation for closing it down. The water lines to the pier were shut off and removed.

"Where's Dad and Garrett? What happened?" he kept repeating to himself.

The shore power cables were disconnected and removed. His head was swimming. He wanted to lie down. Deck hands were untying the lines holding the gangway to the ship.

Up the pier, a taxi was honking its horn and flashing the headlights as it raced toward the ship. In a flurry of dust the cab slid to a stop, George and Garrett hopped out and the cabbie pulled luggage from the trunk. They made it aboard!

They exchanged waves as the quarterdeck crew escorted them inside the ship and the gangway was stowed. Lines pulled in and the ship got underway.

It wasn't until the Navigation Detail secured that Jack was free to find his dad and nephew. It appears that George "took the fall" for Jack by claiming he was driver ... cops took him to the drunk tank where he spent the night ... got arraigned first thing in the morning ... called the office to report the whereabouts of the company car ... made it to the hotel to pack up the grandkid and then jumped a cab to the ship.

Even a couple of prayers from a saint won't undo the damaging combination of no sleep and a lot of booze!

After the dust settled and the booze haze wore off, Jack and George chatted at mid-deck.

"Dad, I can't thank you enough for taking the fall on the DUI."

"That's okay, I couldn't see you go through that and maybe miss the ship or have a problem with the NAVY."

"What happened?" Jack asked.

George began "They booked me and put me in a large common cell with the other drunks. I stayed on my feet most of the time. I told the jailer about the ship leaving early and that I needed to be aboard. They were nice enough to arraign me first."

"I hate to ask ..."

"The judge confiscated my driver's license. So I have to write a letter to get it back. No big deal."

"Well, it's a big deal to me, dad. Thank you."

RE-AWAKENING

It hadn't moved from its slightly tilted posture. It just sat there hunched over and silent, as if waiting for Jack to complete a thought ... resolve some conflict or express a feeling .... It was as if the red hulk itself was baiting him to laugh, cry or lament his past. He felt half-empty. Did he waste half his life with near misses and stupidity? Or was he half-full ... with an enriched slice of life's extreme experiences?

Either way ... he wasn't done. So he decided he was half-full and that his imaginary conversations with God, after every close call, he received encouragement to pick it up and move on. There were good things ahead.

Back state-side, the tired ship was scheduled for an overhaul in Seattle's Puget Sound, the Bremerton NAVY Shipyard. That meant the last nine months of Jack's tour was a "shore-job" ... A beer every night and a bed that didn't move!

He found a little one-bedroom cottage in

Bremerton and wasted no time in calling Samantha to come out for a visit, maybe stay for a week or two. It was a beautiful place. The Bremerton shipyard on the western side of Puget Sound offered vistas of Seattle skyline and Mount Rainier to the east and the pine covered Olympic Mountain range to the west.

She was his personal pinup girl. An instant full color Polaroid photo of her was taped to the inside of his stateroom desk. He greeted her every morning and mentally caressed her every night as he stared at her image.

The girl of his dreams popped out of the photo taped to his stateroom locker and into his arms at SEATAC airport. Before he knew it, the week was over and she was gone. Two days later, his withdrawal pains had him crawling like an addict. He called her in Michigan and suggested that she return and "play house." A week later, her orange Toyota Corolla with a small box trailer were sitting in the driveway when he got off work. He opened the back door and was greeted by Taffy, her cocker spaniel. That very moment, his knees almost buckled when she appeared in the doorway looking like a playboy bunny with her long wavy blond hair cascading over her shoulders in a low cut red dress! Wow! Heaven on earth!

Jack's spunky Tomboy girlfriend evolved into his **best friend and lover**. In a matter of a few days,

Samantha adapted to becoming the Dungeness crab "Bagger" on their scuba dives for "catch-n-cook" dinners.

A NAVY Pacific Region competition was announced open to any regionally located personnel to a downhill Giant Slalom competition to be held at Snoqualmie Ski Resort. More than 35 skiers were listed on a NAVY message as entrants. Jack pulled his 10 year-old Giant Slalom Jean Claude Killy signature VR17 skis last used in High School and got excited to compete again. His goal was to finish in the top ten.

They drove up to Snoqualmie Summit Ski Resort on a cold and very overcast and somewhat windy day. At the competitor briefing in the lodge, the weather conditions were significantly different and a notable concern. Visibility was bad over the Olympic caliber Giant Slalom course and reported to be icy as the falling snow was blowing across the icy course and not sticking or accumulating. Instead, the wind was blowing the flakes off the course altogether. It was announced due to concern for the safety of participants, only two runs were planned as the additional precautions and number of participants slowed the organizers. Samantha armed with a camera captured Jack on film. The result was his tucked image in motion just before the finish line. He finished 11th fastest of those who completed both runs.

Although he had anticipated departing the NAVY, he still owed a car loan balance on the Jaguar XKE and decided to sell it. In its place he bought a 1971 Volkswagen Beetle and modified it with cut down fenders, jacked up shocks, large off-road truck tires and a 6 gallon military style Jerry fuel can on a bracket mounted to the rear bumper.

The little pale yellow bug found first duty driving up the fire roads of the Olympic Mountain Range. Samantha, Taffy and he made frequent weekend trips to sightsee. Samantha wasn't intimidated by anything ... including shooting beer cans in the Olympic Mountains with his 45 cal 1911 model handgun. She turned out to be a good shot, too!

They planned to drive the VW along the coastal roads to San Diego, then deep into Mexico after his decommissioning. He needed to take an extended road trip/vacation before commencing his civilian career and the VW bug was versatile and economical for car camping.

His eyes refocused on the buoy in the fog as these ethereal reminiscences snapped shut at the sounds of splashing. The surface of the bay water transformed from a dull frosted glass to circular ripples like rain drops had fallen. Jellyfish don't break the surface he thought as he peered into the water. Then, it became clear a school of medium-sized Mackerel/Bunkers were streaming eastward toward Flanders Bay.

Another swig of coffee and he was ready for the next tune, "Ain't No Sunshine" by Bill Withers … this time, the little ditty may be used as a flourish at the end.

Ain't no sunshine when she's gone …

"Ba Dip Dat Doodley Doo"

FOREST OF ANGELS

The second in command of a US NAVY ship is the Executive Officer, aka "XO". He oversaw every function of the ship and executed the Captains orders. He wasn't a bad guy, just someone who had to keep things moving as the Captain ordered.

Junior Officers of the Wardroom were beginning to rotate out of their current positions as a fresh batch of newly commissioned Ensigns arrived. In a goodwill gesture, the XO and his wife hosted a "Hail and Farewell" dinner at their house not far from the shipyard. The event commemorated the departure of Officers from Wardroom roster and simultaneously welcomed the arrival of their replacements. The occasion featured speeches, presentations of the Ship's Plaque, reminiscences of note, ports visited and the like. At one point, Jack was describing the size of the coconut crabs and was surprised when Samantha exclaimed that Jack was exaggerating! A roar of laughter broke out as he tried to recover. The inference being that his letter writing was full of overly generous "sizes" of things ... like "man-things".

A little embarrassed, on the walk to the car after they left, he told her he didn't like the upshot comment that seemed to be aimed at making fun of him. The silent car ride back to cottage could have been a foretelling of their future together. He gave it a long thought. When they got to the cottage, he asked her to sit on the couch. She braced herself for the second round of criticism, but he dropped to one knee and asked her to marry him. And she accepted!

Samantha becoming his fiancé triggered a whole new way he thought about the future. Jack's mind was freed from the usual clutter. Everything suddenly became clearer. He was starting anew, like being baptized. His heart and soul became a clean blank sheet of paper and he wanted to be careful what he wrote on it.

In a week or so, they would leave this shipyard town and the NAVY behind. In packing his stuff to go, he came across an envelope of old girl friend photos and his "little black book" of their names, phone #s, addresses, birthdays and similar notes. He didn't want to keep these reminders of his past dalliances of romance. He promptly burned the envelope in an outdoor incinerator.

Samantha saw his actions and pondered upon the envelope's contents. "What was that … old girlfriend letters and stuff?"

"No", he responded, but after a momentary hesitation, he nodded in the affirmative. "Stuff, I no longer need".

"Huh!"Samantha uttered casting a doubtful eye in his direction.

"What girlfriends? There's never been anyone but you. The only space in my heart, is for the one I will spend the rest of my life with ... you" Jack said. She didn't need to know and he wasn't about to disclose. If anytime the topic of past girlfriends comes up, he'll deny there was anyone but her.

To further insulate the subject, he burned the romantic bridges of the past. No more disco dancing Brendas for him, he just gave up. Nothing and no one will come between them.

What followed his change in status from USN "active" to "reserve" was a 6-week 12,000 mile road trip. The first leg was from Seattle down the Pacific Coast Highway to San Diego where her Mother lived. Jack drove back north for a day in Los Angles to get an interview for a motorsports press relations position which sounded promising. It hinted of a career path somewhat like his Dads'. Upon leaving San Diego Sam and Jack resumed a southern direction intending to drive the length of the Baja Peninsula to La Paz. From there, a ferried crossing of the Gulf of California to Mazatlan followed by driving a little further to Puerto Vallarta. They stayed and played in Puerto Vallarta for a few days then got the itch for the road again and soon were wandering the open air market of Guadalajara before continuing to Mexico City. A few days of City highlights and pyramids were enough so they began the long drive north through Monterrey to Dallas, Texas and the eastern seaboard to the Hamptons of Long Island, New York.

Jack and Samantha agreed the six week adventure had ended beautifully. But the job available for Jack was back on the west coast. It was fortuitous that the principal of the motorsports job was currently at the Indianapolis Motor Speedway. Jack had to have a second interview which happened in the back of the Jim Hall/Johnny Rutherford/Pennzoil team RV. He got the job in Los Angeles and had to get there pronto!

Luck was still on his side ... the day the little VW brought him safely to Redondo Beach, he checked in with his new employer, found a small house for rent in San Pedro with a view of the Long Beach/Los Angeles Harbor and convinced the landlord to let him immediately move in with no money!

In the year that followed, he worked in the enviable environment of motorsports. He was honored and humbled by so many notable figures in NASCAR,

INDYCAR/USAC, SCORE and IMSA sanctioned events. He met and worked around famous drivers such as Dale Earnhardt, Richard Childress, Parnelli Jones, Johnny Rutherford, Mario Andretti, Bob Bondurant, Howdy Holmes, Kevin Cogan, Mickey Thompson, Josele Garza, Dan Gurney .... and many others.

He had a great time and it was fun ... but it was a very low paying job. Samantha found work a short distance away from the little house they rented on the hillside of San Pedro. She took the job as a short order cook/counterperson at a local 'Five & Dime' store. Jack, unfortunately, was released from his employment to make room for the principal's son who just graduated college. It happened almost to the day of his anniversary with the firm. It was the beginning of his long arduous trek to find and pursue a career with a future. They were committed to each other and surviving no matter what, after all, they were in love. For awhile, they lived off her tip money kept in a jelly jar in the kitchen cabinet. Needless to say, they were on a tight budget, but they were happy.

Samantha jumped at a hamburger manager job to fill in for the loss of his income contribution. Jack desperately looked for work ... and took stints at an auto body repair shop, residential solar system sales and a few other entry-level jobs. One late night after his sales calls in a nice residential area of Orange County, he found himself counting the change he scrounged from the floor and ash tray to hopefully buy enough gasoline to get home. *What the hell am I doing here?* He suddenly focused on making himself more valuable beyond the Fluffer-Nutter English under-grad degree with some NAVY time.

His big break occurred with an assistant marketing position at a data processing service providing payroll and accounting applications. Using VA benefits, he took night courses to earn an MBA in Marketing & Management Information Systems. Samantha entered the blossoming Los Angeles Aerospace industry through an industrial security job to manage classified publications and documents. She also enrolled in night courses in computer programming and progressed to other aerospace IT positions.

Looking beyond the data processing business, he nailed a junior marketing position in a motorcycle manufacturer's U.S. distribution company in the fall of 1984. Just a few months later, Samantha landed a programmer position at a rival Japanese manufacturer's USA headquarters. Their two new employers were only miles apart.

In the late summer of 1985, Samantha's brother, Greg graduated college and moved nearby. He bought himself a cruiser motorcycle. About the same time, Jack had a company motorcycle, perk of the job. It was a standard but sporty 750. Greg and he had not ridden together much and kept trying to put on some mileage. But, as usual, everyday chores and other things always seemed to get in the way.

Aside from riding the 750 to and from work on a daily basis, Jack did go on a few rides with a couple of guys from the company and a crash prone friend. This motorcycle that Jack was assigned turned out to be bit tall for him. Just sitting on it required using tippy toes to keep it upright and balanced. The motorcycle had a center of gravity higher than Jack expected for a V-twin engine. In addition to his challenge with handling the heavy weight of the bike, was that under hard acceleration, the tail felt light. These effects were in large part muted when Samantha was aboard with him ... the bike sat lower to the ground and he dare not use the "throttle wide open" with her aboard ... yet.

Aside from a handful of mini-bikes, dirt bikes, a 305cc Honda and the Harley, the amount of his riding experience with a passenger was limited.

On a Saturday morning in November, the San Gabriel Mountain range just to the north of the City of Los Angeles was clear and looked like there was snow only at the peaks. Samantha and her brother Greg chatted about how clear the vistas would be and low likelihood of encountering snow on the road ... if they did, they'd simply turn around and come back. The area is known as Angeles National Forest with two main entry points on the south side facing Los Angeles. They chose the popular entry from La Canada Flintridge on State Highway 2, the Angeles Crest Highway.

To get there was a relatively short ride on the freeways. The bikes handled well but were low on fuel upon arrival at the exit ramp from the Foothill Freeway to Angeles Crest Highway. Jack signaled Greg to stop for gas at the station.

"It will be a little bit nippy" Greg said with a dual-arm rubbing gesture.

"We'll go slowly. Wind chill won't be as bad as the ride here was," Jack responded, noting their freeway speed of 75 mph will soon be 45 mph on the mountain roads.

Samantha went to the station's restroom while they refueled the two motorcycle tanks. Other bikes pulled in behind them, presumably to ride the crest also. Jack noticed how much heavier the 750 felt when pulling it off the side stand and pushing it clear of the pumps. Samantha returned and they all bundled up a little more and hopped back in the saddles.

They left the station and headed up the crest.
At four or five miles the road tightened and the
snaky road switchbacks began as they rose in
elevation. At this point, the road surface was clear
and dry, the sky blue and cloudless, and the cool
air was full of pine tree aroma. Greg followed a
modest distance as he wasn't as familiar with
the route. Jack had been up here several times
with his Mustang chasing a friend in his Mustang
a model year newer. The size of the tire patch of
the Mustang is at least ten times greater than any
contact patch of a pair of motorcycle tires. So the
ride pace was slow and steady.

The air got noticeably colder just before reaching
the Mount Wilson Observatory Road. Samantha
snuggled into his back. A few miles further they
passed into another cold pocket at Mount Sally,
but kept on going past Newcomb's Ranch Café.
An average number of cars and bikes were in the
parking lot of the café, but almost no one standing
about. As they passed, the rustic aroma of burning
wood hung in the air. They continued only another
few miles to just before reaching Mount Waterman
Ski Area where the ice and snow defied anyone on
two wheels to continue.

Greg called out as they made a U-turn,*"Hey! Let's
go back to that roadhouse!"*

Jack responded with a thumbs-up gesture.

Newcomb's Café is like the Rock Store on Mulholland Drive. Both are popular spots for motorists to stop, stretch and get libation on otherwise unpopulated stretches of mountain road. Weekenders out for a scenic drive, motorcyclists and car enthusiasts congregate and mingle in the parking lot to talk about their "baby" or the roads. You can expect to see everyone chatting and friendly, low-rider, antique and exotic car owners mixing with the motorcycle crowd of chopper, touring and sport bike riders. It wasn't unusual to see celebrities, musicians, actors or people employed in the entertainment industry talking about something technical to everyday Joe's. The unspoken, unwritten rule is that the acceptable topics are not who someone "'is" or what they "do"; it's about the road, the views and the commonality of the machinery of transportation.

Slotting their bikes among the others, Jack called out, *"Whoa! This is colder than I thought! My knees and hands are frozen!"*

"Yeah, same here! Irish Coffee or Hot Toddy for me!" Greg replied.

"Put me next to the fireplace!" Samantha added.

Stepping inside the café door was like stepping into a sauna. The air was thick and warm. The place was noisy. The perimeter of the bar was three to four people deep. The fireplace was even more unapproachable. About twenty minutes elapsed and they got no closer to the bar or café staff to place an order. Jack got frosted ... the other way.

"This is a waste of time! Let's blow this pop stand and go home to the hot tub and margaritas," Jack blurted. *"Besides,"* he continued, *"we warmed up a little."*

Jack should have checked his attitude before putting the key in the ignition for the ride down. He was pissed. They left Newcomb's and he picked up the pace.

A few miles down the road, the shadows had grown longer and a black gravel or sand had been spread. Only the tire tracks were clear of sand. He noticed a little tail wiggle and head shake of the handlebars crossing the gap between tire tracks. A glance in the mirror showed Greg still there. They came upon a tight right hand corner. Uh-oh, too fast! Entering the corner in the left tire track, he could see the turn tightened even more. Before he could think "decreasing radius" they were over the double yellow line and slippery sliding toward the trench of the oncoming side.

BOOM!

He heard voices but couldn't see.

"Here's one"

"You got that one?"

"Chopper called"

"There's a lot of blood there."

Someone touched his leg, *"Okay in there? Don't move, I'm going to take your helmet off."*

Jack's helmet was rotated up and some light came in. The chin strap was undone. Then his aviator sunglasses were lifted out of the bridge of his nose and removed. He saw Samantha sitting on the ground rubbing her leg and being attended by another paramedic. A moment later his helmet was off.

"Here, hold this to your nose," he said putting a small white towel to Jack's face.

Flashing lights of the CHP cars and paramedic meat wagon made a surrealistic scene. Greg was on the other side of the road next to his motorcycle and another CHP car.

The paramedic checked Jack over, *"No broken bones. Can you stand up?"*

"Yeah," he replied as the paramedic and someone else lifted him to his feet, *"How's my ..."*

"She seems to be okay, too. We're going to put you both in a helicopter and send you to the hospital."

"Okay"

He helped Jack walk a hundred yards or so to the turnout on the right side of the road. A helicopter approached and landed. Jack and Samantha were put inside. The flight to Verdugo Hills Hospital was short.

They were in an ER with side-by-side tables separated by a curtain.

"Hi Samantha," Jack said.

"Hi …. were we in an accident?"

"Yes, but we're going to be okay."he said.

"What happened?"

"We were riding a motorcycle and went off the road."

"Am I okay?"

"Yes, I think so."

"Are you okay?"

"Just a bloody nose. I'm fine," he answered.

"Okay"

A CHP Officer came in the room and asked a series of questions for his report.

An ER doctor came to Jack's table and said, *"Let's take a look at your nose."*

He took the small towel Jack was holding and started to wash off the dried blood from his face.

"What kind of glasses were you wearing when this happened?"

"Wire rimmed aviator style sunglasses."

"Prescription?"

"No. I'm wearing contacts."

"Well, you'll need a coupla stitches. It seems that whatever you hit with your helmet pushed the bridge of the glasses into your nose."

He stitched his nose and placed a bandage over it. He then handed him a wet washcloth. *"Here, there's a lot of blood that ran into your mustache and dried."*

As Jack began cleaning up, he tried to puff his cheek, but the air escaped through his mustache.

He called the doctor over and demonstrated the new airway in his upper lip. The physician lifted Jack's lip over and looked at it inside the mouth. Then the ER guy exclaimed, *"Well! You pushed a tooth through it! More stitches!"*

"Jack, were we in an accident?" Samantha asked.

"Yes, but we're going to be okay."

"What happened?"

"We were riding a motorcycle and went off the road."

"Am I okay?"

"Yes, I think so."

"Are you okay?"

"Yes, better now."

"Okay"

She went silent for a few minutes. Jack asked a nurse to pull back the curtain so they could see each other and talk. The curtain was opened and he could see gauze bandages covering each of her knees.

"Where are we?"

"We're in a hospital."

"Why? Did we have an accident?"

"We were riding a motorcycle and slid into a ditch."

"Am I okay?"

"Yes"

"Are you okay?"

"I think so."

"Okay"

The conversation alarmed him to the possibility that he broke Samantha! And that this may be only the beginning of a lifetime answering the same six questions ... over and over and over again. Someone came to tell them the guy they were riding with had left to get his car and will be back for them.

"Samantha, Greg *went home to get his car to pick us up to go home"* he said.

"My brother?"

"Yes, Greg was riding with us."

"Is he okay?"

"Yes, Greg is okay."

"Where are we?"

"We're in a hospital."

"What happened?"

"We were riding a motorcycle and went off the road."

"Am I okay?"

"Yes, I think so."

"Are you okay?"

Right then another doctor came in and spoke with Jack about Samantha's condition.

"She's suffered a significant concussion. The next 24 to 48 hours will tell if there's follow on therapy needed. Here's some instructions. Are you going to be with her the whole time?"

He nodded yes.

"Have an adult with you for the next 24 hours.

Wake her up every one and a half hours tonight. Don't let her sleep any longer than that. If there are any changes for the worse, take her to an ER tonight. See should see her regular doctor in 2 days."

"Okay, I've got it."

Back home, every hour and a half, Jack sewed his bad karma "guilty me" blanket. He not only almost snuffed himself out, he almost took her out too!

DOOM DUNES

The ski trip was organized by Greg's close friend, Bob who had a connection with the condo owner. The owner was more than happy to have the three couples, including their Rottweiler Argus, in the three bedroom suite. This last snowfall was heavy and may have stretched the skiing season another month. The condo was at the base of the mountain, easily within reach of the slopes so that at the end of the day, getting back was a ski-up. Greg and Bob liked the extreme sections of the Advanced Slope that ended at the condo. The rest of them kept to the more humble Intermediate Slopes. The routine had them all start the last run together from the top. Part way down the mountain, Greg and Bob split off for the challenging but shorter run, while the rest of them took the longer gentler trails. Greg has a full head of curly blond hair atop his tall and lanky frame.

He worked up a sweat hopping around in the heavy wet snow of the mogul section. He removed the knit cap. By the end of the run his hair had frozen into Medusa-like snakes. His best buddy, Bob, a little shorter, heavier and had straight brown hair. He also had a "snow halo." The two standing together presented a comical study of contrasts.

Approaching the condo, the telltale sign of skis planted in the snow bank next to the condo hot tub, told the others that Greg and Bob already made it back. Inside, they had already switched to swimsuits, toked and imbibed a couple of beers.

Jack took Argus outside for a walk around the parking lot while the others changed. After Argus marked all the yellow snow spots already surrounding the cars and trucks, they returned to an empty condo as the hot tub was full of activity. By the time he joined the crew in the hot tub, the party was well on the way.

It was the last night of a four day weekend of skiing at Mammoth Mountain. Everyone planned to leave early the next morning for the long drive south on the 395 to Los Angeles.

"I'm going inside for more beer," Jack announced. *"Anyone need a refill?"*

Two "Yes" and three "No"… answers split along the gender line. Guys were into the IPA's and the girls were sticking to their wine. Standing barefoot on the cedar decking next to the tub, he knew he'd be shivering in another 30 seconds in the 25-degree air.

"Pass me the empties," Jack said. Samantha's brother, Greg handed him a beer bottle, but his new best buddy, Bob, hung on to his.

"I'll come in with you," Barbara said, climbing out of the bubbling hot tub water. Bob's girlfriend du jour, a petite brunette, hopped out and bolted for the sliding glass door. Argus was watching them on the other side of the glass. As Jack followed her into the rental condo, he couldn't help but notice her bikini bottoms steaming.

Inside the door, she gave the Rottweiler a pat on the head. *"Good boy, Argus"* she said, and then quickly headed to the bathroom on the other side of the kitchen. She looked over her shoulder and said *"He's such a sweet dog."*

"Thanks," Jack responded, *"and he likes you, too."*

Out of the refrigerator, he pulled the six pack carton with three bottles in it. The girls had more wine, but this was the last of the beer.

Barbara returned and noticed the shortage of male beverage, *"Why not tequila shots?"* she offered.

"Yeah," he said, *"Why not."* Quervo Gold was not the premium tequila he would have preferred to do by the shot glass, but these were desperate times.

She opened the refrigerator door and pulled out two limes. Then a quick tip-toe to the cutting board went about the process of cutting the lime wedges.

"Salt," she said, *"over there"* pointing to the salt shaker on the countertop. *"But I'll bring it since your carrying beer, a bottle and cups."*

"Brrrr!" he exclaimed crossing the patio to the hot tub. His feet were cold and the tub water welcomed them back with a little burning sensation.

"Barbara," Bob asked, *"are you having fun yet?"*

"I will, once I get back in there." She was covered in goose bumps and climbed in quickly followed by an audible sigh of relief. *"Yes! I'm having a great time!"*

"Me too!"

"Absolutely!"

"Yep!"

"You got that right," Sandy, Greg's girlfriend said.

"Me, too," Jack added, *"it's unanimous!"*

The night sky was partially clouded and stars poked through between them.

"Did anyone catch the forecast for more snow?"Greg asked.

"I know what you're thinking … maybe we can get snowed-in and stay longer?" Jack asked.

"Well, yeah …"Greg confessed. "None of us used chains getting here. It snowed after we arrived."

"They're not gonna buy that back at HQ!"he scolded. "Besides, I don't have a break in my schedule or any more accumulated time off."

"Nope."

"Not me."

"I went into the vacation hole just to make it this time," Barbara said.

"Well let's do something next weekend, then" Bob suggested.

"Like what? Right now, we're outta money," Jack said, "Whatever it is, has to be low cost and … dog friendly."

"Do you have dirt bikes?" Bob asked.

"No, but I may be able to borrow one … or two" Jack answered.

Greg looked at Jack. He was about to answer him when his girlfriend, Sandy spoke up, *"No Greg! I'm not going to ride on one of those things! I'm not healed from the last time."*

It was a three-wheeled ATV that they took to San Felipe last Memorial weekend. She rode as a passenger and got her butt burned when Greg flipped it. She was trapped and the hot muffler branded her butt on the left cheek.

The vivid memory of her screaming at Greg to get it off and his slow deliberative pace in responding would have been funny if it wasn't real ... and painful.

"Ahh, well I can't get a 3-wheeler anymore. Those were replaced with 4-wheelers. They aren't as easy to tip," Jack said.

"Have you been to Pismo?" Bob asked.

"No, what's Pismo?" Jack asked

"Miles and miles of sand dunes right on the ocean! Cheap, easy to get to and we can camp overnight." Bob enthusiastically offered.

"I'm out," said Barbara.

"Leave early Saturday morning and return Sunday afternoon?" Jack asked.

"*We could do that,*" Greg said.

He looked to Samantha for her take on it. She gave a nod of approval. Sandy wasn't so sure, but would probably go along if Greg pushed her.

"*Jack, we decided to get together and camp at Pismo next weekend*", Greg announced.

"*Yeah,*" said Bob, "*dirt biking and riding ATV's on the beach and sand dunes, you game?*"

"*We're talking Saturday and Sunday, right?*" Jack confirmed.

"*That's the plan, man!*" Greg replied.

"Not as involved as going to San Felipe," Greg responded, "Less driving time, one night there, less gear to take, and about a day's worth of riding."

San Felipe was their coveted spot on the eastern side of the Mexican Baja Peninsula on the Gulf of California,. And Memorial Day weekend was their favored time to be there, because of the long distance driving involved each way. Pismo Beach, a lot closer, is midway between San Luis Obispo and Santa Maria. He had never been to Pismo, but heard about it. The Off Highway Vehicle Park is the very last location where vehicles were allowed to drive on a beach in California and camping in the dunes is great.

Considering all of them were working stiffs and couldn't ask for more time off at such short notice. A weekend overnighter seemed like a good idea.

"Okay," Jack said, *"count us in! I can't drive the Mustang on the beach, so we'll need to ride with you guys."*

"That's what I was thinking," Greg said, *"Can you get some ATVs?"*

"I've got a trailer, I can put my dirt bike in the pickup bed, so we can put them on my trailer for the round trip," said Bob.

"I'll see what I can do," Jack responded.

Monday, back in the office, he wasted no time in sourcing and arranging for two quad ATVs a small 200 cc unit and a 300 cc model. Arrangements were made for Bob to meet Jack at work and load them on his trailer at 5:00 pm Friday. The plan was to meet in the morning for breakfast, then caravan the 3 hours up California Highways 1 and 101 to the Pismo Beach exit just past Oceano.

A sign announced Oceano Dunes State Vehicular Recreation Area at the entrance to Pismo. A little further was the Park Sentry gate. Entering the park, all vehicles are advised to lower the air pressure in the tires for driving on sand. After dropping tire pressure, they then headed south along the oceans waterline on a long slow drive to the dunes/camping area, then continued around the perimeter of open dune area. A camp spot was located on the east side of a large cluster of sand dunes sculpted by wind.

There were no foot prints or tire tracks as the constant westerly breeze fills them in and carves a new dune shape with each slight shift in wind direction. The dunes featured steep slopes, called slip drops were mostly on the Eastern side of the sand mounds. In a slip drop of a huge dune, we found the best wind protection to pitch our tents and arrange them around a fire pit.

Saturday afternoon ride around..... a noisy group of young ruffians pitch their two tents next to them. Their pickup had all four doors loaded with speakers fully open and pumping out loud rock. They wasted no time in being as loud as possible, perhaps with hopes anyone else would tire of them and move away. At dusk, the dune driving is shutdown and they gathered about the fire pit with a few beers. The heavy drinking and noise increased next door to them and continued after they turned in for the night. At around 2 am they awakened to the sound of banging metal pots and pans. Jack, Greg and Bob confronted the noisy ones and were drunkenly rebuffed, but they did quiet a little for the next two hours. The need for pot-banging self-expression ceased at about 4am.

At about 6am Sunday morning, Jack, Greg and Bob were ready to start the day with a beach ride and a detour into town for breakfast burritos. As a courtesy wakeup to the noisy neighbors, Samantha started the small quad engine and revved it to "warm it up."

Samantha takes off with a rooster tail of airborne sand, while Jack goes about refilling the fuel tank on the 300cc quad. He estimated she had a good four minute lead heading due west to the ocean. Jack also left the campsite with a sand rooster tail, a little thank you to the inconsiderate neighbors.

He followed in the general direction that Samantha took, but her ATV tracks in the sand blended with those of others. Then, Jack finds he's on a dune with no tire tracks. Minutes later, he spots Samantha just sitting on the ATV at the top of a tall dune. Jack made a bee-line toward her ... and straight into a sudden slip drop. It was a huge bowl that went deep and he was all too late braking ... his reaction slowed the 400 pound machine as it slipped over the edge. A ledge or bowl shelf appeared two-thirds of the way to the bottom.

No airtime, just rapid drop where ATV slammed head-first into shelf. The ATV stopped, but he kept going and took the first hit in the chest by the right handlebar. "Ooommph" He flew like Superman after that and landed face down at the bottom. Almost instantly, the ATV landed on top of him and took the last of the air from his lungs. "Hunnn … eehh"

Luckily the seat part of the ATV hit his upper back. If it was any other part of the machine landing on him would have been really, really bad. As it was, he's pinned facedown. His right arm, tightly held below was unmovable. He couldn't breathe … couldn't move … he was trapped! Face buried in sand, though goggles did help, his squirming to get out only seemed to tighten more. Sand was in his ears, hair and mouth. BUT HE COULDN'T INHALE! It felt like a total body seizure struggling to gasp the tiniest amount of air … like trying to breathe through a hypodermic needle.

Left arm could move only a little. Rolling to the right, he could move it a few inches. Repeating the movement of rolling to the right and inching the left arm out from underneath made a tiny bit of progress each time.

Left arm finally free, he pushed sand out from under his head. "Oh shit, I'm gonna die this time!"

Then he smelled the gasoline and felt a rivulet of
the stuff running down a leg. Still not breathing,
the urgency to get from under the ATV turned to
panic. Kicking ... wriggling ... twisting ....pushing
sand ... took forever to crawl out from under the
machine. The weight removed made no difference
to the constricting muscles that prevented air into
his lungs.

He turned slightly to see the top of Samantha's
whip flag above the next dune. She was so close
and yet too far. He couldn't make a sound ... there
was no horn on the ATV, he couldn't utter a sound,
and nothing to bang together.

Free but still on his knees, he cannot gulp the
tiniest amount of air ... about 4 or 5 minutes ...
how long had it been? ...was he gonna die? Diving
training taught him that an asphyxiation death can
happen in as little as 3 minutes.

Moments later he was on the verge of passing-out
when his throat loosened a little to get only the
trickle of air at first. He tried to call to Samantha.
Each time he did, the whip flag waved a little.
Several additional attempts to call, he couldn't
get loud enough, just laid there ... breaths short ...
about 15 minutes later he could breath better. Back
at camp ... Samantha thought she heard someone
... looked around but saw no one. Jack had a big
bruise on his chest ... the ATV had a bent handlebar.

He tried to straighten the handlebars but couldn't by himself. He called to Samantha for help.

"Are you okay?" she asked. "This thing is really bent."

"It only hurts when I laugh."

"You've got to be more careful. You have to last a long time!" she said, then gave him a hug.

"Ahhh!" he said, "A little too tight."

She loosened her grip. "What were you doing?"

"Trying to catch up to you."

Her eyes squinted with a stern look. "LOOK BEFORE YOU LEAP! You're driving too fast in an unfamiliar area. You have to last another 30 years."

"Okay"

HAVE A HEART

It was March 2003 in California, right after the very sad passing of Samantha's brother, Greg. A restless Saturday night as Jack mulled clips in his memory of the last time he and Greg were together, an unpleasant scene as he succumbed to injuries from an auto accident with a drunk driver. Tossing and turning the few hours in bed was not restful. Eyeing the clock on the nightstand read 4:03 AM. At that point, he became aware that his mouth was dry, sinuses clogged and breathing was laborious. Sitting up on the side of the bed a few minutes, he felt better but sleep was still out of the question. Not wanting to disturb the slumbering bodies of Samantha and Argus next to him, he left the bedroom and clicked on a 24-hour news channel.

It was a Saturday morning and they usually arose about 9 AM. Argus woke him by licking his face. He had fallen asleep sitting upright with the tv on. Argus walked to the sliding patio door and scratched at the glass indicating he wanted to go out. Complying, Jack got up and the two of them climbed the three sets of steps to the top of their backyard.

Jack felt really tired and more than a little winded. Convinced the lack of solid sleep and the beginnings of an ass-kicking sinus cold, he planned to get the most powerful OTC meds at the pharmacy when it opened.

"Don't bother!" she said, *"Go to the walk-in at the hospital and get some real drugs. You'll get over whatever you've got much faster."*

He left Samantha and Argus at home while he drove to the clinic. The Jaguar XKE sitting in the garage was his target project for the day and he wanted to get his sinuses and the headache cleared up. It turned out that the walk-in clinic was the Emergency Entrance to Torrance Memorial; they were one and the same. He described his symptoms to the inquisitive young nurse as she pumped the blood pressure bladder on his arm, she abruptly said *"Stay right here."*

Before he knew it, he was on a table in the Emergency Room getting things pasted to his torso and wired up. A short time later, Samantha walked into the curtained space with a tall, slim good looking elderly gentleman, Dr. Harold Santana, the Cardiologist on-call.

Jack re-told the story of sleeplessness and climbing the stairs with Argus.

"So, can I go now?" he asked, feeling somewhat agitated.

"No, you're not going anywhere" the doctor said. Both Samantha and the physician's eyes were focused on the monitor above Jacks head. *"A hundred seventy-nine ... we're keeping you right here for observation and some tests."*

"What? Hey, I've got stuff to do."

*"You are a very sick man! Why did you wait so long to come here?"*the cardiologist asked.

"I didn't know anything was wrong ... just a sinus headache and fatigue!"

"You're lucky you did ... any longer could have been fatal. Just relax," he said as their eyes remain fixed on the red line and numbers on the screen above his head.

The doctor left the curtain room abruptly. Samantha gave him a disapproving look and shook her head.

"I didn't know ... you know I'm not the kind of guy to puss-out on stuff."

She didn't say much but the image of her smirk and head shake lingered after she left to go home to their awaiting Argus. He was later told his condition was Congestive Heart Failure and his lungs were filling with fluid, hence the labored breathing and fatigue.

Jack was released from the hospital on Monday. Samantha left work early that day to pick him up. Needless to say, he was under her strict supervision going into the series of frequent visits to Dr. Santana's. The condition was atrial fibrillation, whereas the heart quivers and doesn't do the bump-thump of a healthy heart.

During these weekly visits, the doctor addressed him as "Young Man", although he's 49 years young. Each week he would make a very slight adjustment of the Warfarin dosage, repetition of instructions to take walks for exercise and to return the following week. His blood had to be thinned within a narrow range for the next stage, but it was always slightly above or below. Diet was the determining element that pushed it out of the tiny target range. It went on for months and Jack was losing his cool. The nurse taking the blood sample wasn't happy to see him and his attitude for another go around. She finally spoke to the doctor about her displeasure of dealing with him.

That day they had a break-through in their consultation.

"How did I get to this condition? I'm not a smoker, not overweight, not diabetic, don't use drugs, don't have high blood pressure … I exercise regularly, eat and sleep well …"

"By process of elimination …" the doctor pondered aloud, *"… it could have been caused by a virus."*

"A virus!" Jack stammered, *"So, I could have touched something and then touched my face?"*

His nod and shoulder shrug confirmed it. He was studying the blood results report with the warfarin dosage.

"What the heck!" the doctor announced, *"we'll do it anyway!"*

A few days later, Jack arrived back at the hospital for the procedure called "electrical cardio version". As he got a gurney ride into the cold OR, Samantha walked alongside and he studied her face.

"What?" she asked.

"If I don't make it, you'll find me at Saint Peters gate with the pups waiting."

"You're not getting out of this that easy!"

An intravenous injection worked fast and he was

out. No white light … no young guy with a beard and stone tablets … no fencing or gates … He woke up to Samantha's face close to his own.

"That was interesting!" she whispered, *"they tried to get me to leave, but I wouldn't. I wanted to watch."*

"Really? What happened?"

"Dr. Santana zapped you and your heart stopped! Then a few seconds later, he zapped you again and it started a normal rhythm!"

"Whoa! So, I was dead for a few seconds?"

"Yeah, but that's not the interesting part. When he shocked you the second time, your right arm raised up and moved back and forth like you were conducting an orchestra."

"That's probably why I didn't get to hear the angels singing … the band intro was interrupted!" he quipped.

"He said you're going to have to take it easy for awhile, or you could go backwards."

"Crumb! I want to get outta here," he complained. Dr. Santana came bed side and said that he'll have to follow up with him for at least 6 months. Maybe,

just maybe, if he's good and things look normal then, he'll have a one year checkup and that will be the end of it.

Jack disappointed that his near death experience didn't offer a glimpse of "the other side", he focused on being good ... very good.

THE POND

Grayness all around … 360 degrees of grayness and above as well, only the dull red buoy solemnly floating in front of him. The little aluminum boat seemed to drift around it. Jack looked at the waterline of the buoy and noted the little swirls as the tide must be coming back into the bay. It gave him a sense of direction how to get back to the pond.

He stood up to blow the horn a last time before leaving his solemn audience, a slow and somewhat growly version of Harlem Nocturne. It was his favorite tune, but this time his imaginary band mates weren't playing.

He played the two phrases slowly:

"Baa dip datt doodily doo"

"Baa dip datt doodily doodily doo"

Interrupted by sounds of splashing water, the school of Bunkers returned and aggressively fed.

The fish were breeching the water's glassy surface. He wondered if Samantha would be agreeable to waking up and returning with him to fish. It was only a few days ago that she complained about the lack of angler action in pond's channel. Whatever she caught would become the bait for her crab traps that she'd drop at selected spots in the pond. Her crab trappings were Blue Claw with a spider crab occasionally in the mix.

She was smart, practical and stubborn yet quirky and innovative but not prone to impulsiveness, he inwardly smiled upon his good fortune at marrying her. Samantha was his everything ... equal partner, best friend, confidant, advisor and lover.

Just then, he realized that something was missing ... he wanted to play something else but there was no song that came to him. He picked up the sax to blow it again anyway ... put it to his lips but didn't make a note ... just the air hiss as it went passing over the reed and through the horn. He unclipped the neck strap from the horns body and placed the instrument back in the safety of the orange life preserver.

A glance at the water swirling past the buoy hinted at the direction of home. A moment later the engine started and he headed in the general direction of the Cold Creek Pond inlet. The motor smoothly hummed as he looked back over his shoulder at the buoy fading into the fog and then it was gone. The sun began to erase some of the fog overhead, but the moisture beaded on his face as his eyes strained to make out the channel markers.

He wasn't looking forward to the wake that evening for Aunt Martha but, he did want to catch up with his cousins. It had been almost a decade since they last met.

Just ahead, the green channel post slowly emerged from the fog. It held the sign "No Wake, 5 MPH, Radar Enforced". He throttled back the little outboard motor to a crawl. The pond meant many things to him ... safe harbor, wildlife refuge, provider of tasty clams, crabs and a swimming challenge! Halfway through the channel, a pair of white geese was feeding in the slack tide calmness.

Ahead at the public boat launch, a sailboat was having its mast stepped by three men and a woman. As he drew closer, he could hear them talking. One unmistakable voice was his sister, Lisa. He drew close enough to hail her and discovered that two of the men were delivering her new twenty-foot Cat Boat and the other fellow was her son, Jett. After a few moments, Jack restarted the engine and picked his way through the boats buoy moored, to his dock on the opposite side of the pond.

He turned the boat engine off and glided to the floating dock. A quick tie-up, he grabbed the saxophone, coffee cup and walked back to the barn house. After hanging the sax in its place on the wall, he poured another cup of coffee. He peeked from the bedroom doorway to see Argus raise his head in greeting and Samantha's angelic face wake and smile at him.

All at once it hit him, everything else, didn't matter.